Thank you so much for your support! – India

THE RED ROOM

INDIA NORFLEET

The Red Room

Copyright © 2013 by India T Norfleet-Lewis.

Published by:

Erotic Servings Publishing LLC.

Roseville Michigan, USA 48066

Chapter One

Mona leaned against the red wall in front of the floor-to-ceiling window in her office, glanced up toward the breathtaking Detroit skyline, and sighed heavily. Not even the beautiful view of the sunny summer morning and smell of freshly baked cinnamon rolls from the bakery across the street could bring a smile to her face. For the past six months, many of her mornings had been spent in her own private world of gloom and sadness, and she blamed Shaun Harper. He was the one responsible for the pain now festering in her heart. Every year around the time of what would've been their anniversary, Mona fell into a deep depression and blamed herself for Shaun's behavior.

Walking away from the window, Mona grabbed a tissue from her desk and dabbed at the tears forming in her big brown eyes. Perching herself on the matching ottoman in front of her lounger, she reached for her cell phone, tapped the text icon, and immediately went to the last text message she received from Shaun.

"Sorry bastard didn't even have the decency to break up with me in person," Mona whispered as she read the six-month-old text for the millionth time.

Mona Lisa, things are moving too fast for me right now. I'm still trying to have fun and enjoy my prime years. Being tied down to one woman is not something I desire for at least the next five years, if then. So, it's only right that I not waste any more of your time or lead you on to believe in something that is never going to happen. I care for you too much to hurt you any more than I have already. Have a nice life, beautiful, and if you can, please find it in your heart to forgive me for the way I've ended things.

Shaun

Looking at the screen spotted with her tears, Mona's thumb hovered over the delete button for the millionth time since their break up, but this time, she followed through with pressing delete. She had been going through these same motions every year around this time but never had the courage to let go and move on. Instantly, a message popped up on the screen.

Are you sure you want to delete this message?

Mona thought back on the two-year relationship she had with Shaun and couldn't help but let the corners of her lips curl into a genuine smile. It had been two of the best and most memorable years of her 33 years of life. Shaun was everything she'd ever wanted in a man. He'd proved it many times during their courtship, which is one of the reasons why she was still taking the split so hard, even though it had been three years since that dreadful night. She had so many questions she needed answered, but when he refused to even acknowledge her after the way he ended things, Mona lost all hope in getting the closure she so desperately wanted.

Wiping her eyes, Mona glanced down at the screen and read the alert again. Holding her finger over the yes box, she went to press the button. However, at the last second, she pressed no, and clicked on his number instead. She pushed the speakerphone button and waited for the call to connect.

After ringing once, an automated voice said, "I'm sorry, but the number you have reached is no longer in service. Please check your call and dial again."

"No, it can't be. His number has never been disconnected before."
Mona was panic-stricken as she hit redial. When the same message played, she ended the call and went into delayed shock.

"I guess it's really over, but it wasn't supposed to end like this. It wasn't supposed to end."

Mona threw her phone across the room, scooted onto her lounger, and cried uncontrollably.

"He never loved me," she screamed between sobs. "All I ever wanted was to be loved."

.

Chapter Two

"Excuse me. Hello?" said the sexy stranger who seemed to appear from thin air.

"Hello. How can I be of assistance today?" Mona asked.

"Is the owner available?"

"That depends on who's asking," Mona replied, while taking in the physical characteristics of the six-foot, five-inch sexy piece of chocolate with the fresh lineup, hazel eyes, and runner's body.

"Carter Valentine of The Wellmen's Real Estate Group," he replied.

"I'm the owner, Mona Cartwright. What is this concerning?" Mona inquired as she tried to hide her naughty thoughts and instant sexual attraction to this very handsome man.

"You're the owner?" Carter was completely shocked.

"Yes, I am."
"Why don't you have a current picture posted on your business

bio?"

"Because I love the element of surprise. Now, what can I do for you? I'm a very busy woman," Mona stated, tapping her nails on the sign-in log.

"Is it okay if we go somewhere and talk in private?"

Your place or mine, sexy? Stop it, Mona.

"I suppose so, but I'll need you to sign in, and I'll have to hold your ID while you're on my premises."

Mona continued to maintain her nonchalant attitude, although inside, she couldn't think of anything other than the multiple positions she wanted to imitate with this stranger.

After he handed over his driver's license and the sign-in sheet, Mona slid everything in the top drawer behind the hostess station and then said, "Follow me."

They started down a long, wide, gray hallway dimly lit by a string of skylights above framed, hand painted, erotic art of flawless beautiful couples of all ethnicities. As they neared their destination, Carter found it extremely difficult to concentrate on anything but Mona's perfect curves and long model legs as her hips and shapely ass cheeks swayed back and forth in a very seductive, almost hypnotizing rhythm.

Mona finally turned left at the end of the hallway and then entered a door leading into a massive office that had sensual deep red and black walls and decor.

"Please, Mr. Valentine, have a seat." Mona extended her hand toward the two red wingback chairs positioned in front of her desk.

"Thank you."

"No problem. Now, let's get down to business. What is the reason for your visit today?"

"Wow! You're not one to beat around the bush, I see," Carter laughed.

Damn, even his laugh is sexy, Mona noticed before shaking off the thought.

"No, not at all, especially when it keeps me from running my business effectively, Mr. Valentine."

"Please, call me Carter, and you're absolutely right. So, let me get straight to the point. My company, The Wellmen's Group, would like to offer you a very hefty sum to buy out your establishment and turn it into a café."

"I'm sorry, Mr. Carter, but Soothing Touch is not for sale. What gave you the impression that it was?" Mona smiled tightly. *He's not so fine after all, fucking jerk.*

"Well, your business records are public domain, and being the owner of a real estate company, I am privy to a more detailed report. I know your massage parlor business is bringing in an impressive amount of money, but you're not doing nearly as well as you were when you first opened seven years ago."

"Mr. Valentine--"

"Please, call me Carter."

"I'd rather call you a son of a female dog, but I am trying to be nice, Mr. Valentine. Furthermore, please do not step into my place of business and insult me, when you know nothing about owning a massage parlor. Especially one I put my blood, sweat, and tears into and spent years in school preparing for, which allows me to run a safe, legit, and very profitable parlor. My business is doing fine and is absolutely not for sale."

"Mona...may I please call you Mona?"

"No, you may not."

"Fine. Ms. Cartwright, I would strongly advise you to consider my offer. Everyone who has refused my company went belly up after I tried to save their businesses."

"Mr. Valentine, my business does not need saving nor has it ever. And are you threatening me?" Mona asked as she stood and crossed her arms over her very ample breasts.

"Ms. Cartwright, I would never threaten you. I'm just merely informing you, as I have been down this road plenty of times before."

"Well, as you know, I have been running this business for seven years and can assure you that I know exactly what I'm doing."

"Ms. Cartwright, I strongly advise--"

"Mr. Valentine, my business is not for sale, and this conversation is over."

"Ms.--"

"Over, Mr. Valentine."

"Well, thanks for your time anyway. It was definitely a pleasure," Carter said as he stood, straightened his suit jacket, and headed toward the door.

"I'm sure it was. Good day, Mr. Valentine."

"Thank you, even though I know you don't really mean it. For you to be the owner of something called Soothing Touch, you don't have a very soothing personality. Oh well, maybe you'll be more soothing the next time we meet."

"You are sadly mistaken if you think I'll ever speak to you again about this matter."

"Don't be so sure about that. Oh, and by the way, I really hope you're running a legit business, because I intend to do everything I can to acquire this property, including checking to see if massages are really all your establishment is giving out."

"Leave now, Mr. Valentine, before I happily have you thrown out."

"Ms. Cartwright."

Carter finally exited Mona's office. Had he stood there one moment longer spouting his bull, he might've ended up wearing her desk lamp.

"Pompous bastard."

Mona was seething as she heard laughter on the other side of the door before Carter exited the parlor. Walking over to her camouflaged black fridge, Mona pulled out a bottle of Barefoot Red Moscato, pulled the cork, and drank straight from the bottle. She then moved across the room to her red chaise lounge and slid her tired body into the seat as she continued to sip from the bottle while juggling the cork in her perfectly manicured hand. She was pissed off at Carter and utterly exhausted from trying to keep her business out of the red. However, the rude, yet very sexy, asshole was right.

Soothing Touch wasn't doing half as well as it was when Mona first started the business seven years ago. The economy, which was now so depressing, had almost beaten Soothing Touch to a bloody death, especially in the first two years following the recession. Thanks to a silent partner, who Mona had since bought out, a state fair, and a couple months of airtime, Soothing Touch was able to stay afloat. However, all the sleepless nights of worrying over her business and her lack of a personal life were definitely beginning to take their toll.

"Maybe I should let Carter buy me out and go see the world."

Mona considered the thought as she set the half empty bottle of wine on the hardwood floor next to her. Ever since she was a young girl, she had always wanted to travel the world, but she pushed that dream aside to follow her first love, owning a full service parlor.

Be careful what you ask God for, Mona thought as she smiled to herself.

After sulking in her pity a few minutes more, she put the wine away and got back to work. After 12 long, hectic hours later, Mona locked up the parlor and headed home.

Mona was a couple of minutes from home. As she turned the corner a few blocks from her street, her purse slid off the passenger seat. At the same time, her phone began ringing. Choosing to ignore the call until she arrived home, she left her purse on the floor. But, the continued ringing of her cell had her concerned. So, she slowed her speed and began reaching for her purse. Because her purse was too far from her grasp, she would have to pull her seatbelt away from her body, long enough to grab her bag. So, after checking to make sure no vehicles were in her path in case she swerved into another lane, she pulled her seatbelt and leaned across the seat until she hooked her purse and retrieved her phone.

Distracted, she didn't see the Jaguar pulling out of a parking space in front of her. Mona tried to brake hard and swerve, but it was too late. Mona collided with the back of the midnight blue car.

****

"Are you okay?" a familiar voice asked, but Mona couldn't place it as she sat in her car trembling and in tears.

"Yes," Mona sobbed as she held her neck with one hand and pushed the deployed airbag away from her at the same time.

The once soothing voice then yelled, "Good! Just checking to make sure you're well enough to stand up in court."

Still crying, Mona climbed out of her car, and with shaky legs, she approached the guy assessing his damaged vehicle.

"I am so sorry. I will pay for everything."

"You're damn rig--" The driver of the Jaguar stopped mid-sentence after taking a look at the driver who had collided into him. "Mona?"

"Oh my God, Carter! I am so sorry," Mona cried as she inspected his car.

With his car in really bad shape, Carter's jaw twitched as he stood next to a very distraught Mona trying to hold in his anger. He wanted so badly to be upset with Mona for wrecking his ride, but he already knew his strong attraction to her would prevent him from ever dragging her to court. To make matters worse, Carter was a sucker for tears. Especially tears from a woman who he hadn't been able to shake from his thoughts since leaving her office and who he wanted more than a kid wants toys on Christmas morning.

"Mona, calm down. Please stop crying."

"But I wrecked your car, and I know it's going to cost a shit load of money to re--"

"Mona, listen, are you okay?" Carter asked sincerely.

"Yes, I'm fine, but--"

"Then calm down. You don't have to have my car repaired, but only under one condition..."

"Carter, I know I wrecked your car, but my business is still not for sale. You know what? Just sue me, you bastard," Mona spat angrily as she slowly headed back to her car.

"Mona, that's not how I do business, and that's certainly not what I was about to say. The condition is that you have to have dinner with me," Carter said, quickly catching up to her.

Mona paused, contemplating Carter's offer as she leaned on the hood of her Caddy that only had paint missing in a few places.

"Is that all? Just have dinner with you and I don't have to pay to get your car repaired?"

"Correct."

"No funny business?"

"Well, not unless…" Carter laughed when he saw the disgusted look on her face. "No funny business," he finally said.

"Fine. Can I get that in writing?"

"Absolutely."

"Then you got yourself a deal." Mona smiled genuinely for the first time that day.

Chapter Three

Ever the workaholic, Mona staggered into work early the next morning and got right down to business. After opening up her office door wide enough to toss her purse and workbag on the floor, she went to the supply closet and began ordering supplies, then checked staff orders and appointments. She was much more sore from the accident than she realized, and as a result, she ended up canceling all of her appointments for the rest of the day and the next morning. When a bolt of pain shot through her side as she stood up from the receptionist station, she quickly concluded if the pain worsened, she would have to pay her doctor a visit that evening.

By 10 o'clock, the parlor was in full swing. The waiting room was overflowing with customers, and every masseuse's room was occupied. Despite being so busy she couldn't sneak away for a 15-minute break to grab something to eat, she was very pleased with the day's constantly increasing numbers. Therefore, she kept working, ignoring her hunger pangs.

It wasn't until a quarter after four that Mona was finally able to grab a bite to eat. Making a beeline straight for her office, Mona dashed inside and locked the door behind her. While practically running over to her refrigerator to grab the leftover pot roast, potatoes, and hot water cornbread, a flash of red in the direction of her desk caught her eye, causing her to stop dead in her tracks. Turning her head to the left, Mona's breath caught at the sight of what looked to be about three dozen roses sitting in a royal blue vase in the middle of her desk.

"What in the..."

Rushing over to the flowers, Mona grinned as she pulled out the card neatly tucked in the center of the floral arrangement.

"Mmmmm, what are you up to with your sexy self, Mr. Valentine?"

Hello, Mona Lisa. Hope all is well. I've matured quite a bit since our relationship ended, and only thought it fair to apologize to you like the man that I am now and not the child that I was. My new cell is on the back of this card. Please give me a call so I can make things right.

Shaun

Dropping the card, Mona stumbled backward and luckily fell right into the wingback chair behind her. She couldn't believe Shaun was finally reaching out to her. *But why now?*

she wondered. Examining the flowers as if they were contaminated, a million thoughts began racing through her mind. *Does he want me back? If so, why? Is he dying? Does he want my forgiveness? What does he want with me?*

Grabbing the edge of her desk, Mona sat herself upright and touched one of the roses. They were beautiful and absolutely flawless. Mona wondered why Shaun had sent her such a personal gift instead of just mailing a letter. She wanted to know what he was up to before she responded to him. And why for the first time in a little over three years wasn't she looking forward to seeing Shaun or listening to a single thing he had to say?

Before she could ponder her dilemma a second more, her receptionist buzzed.

"Ms. Cartwright, a Carter Valentine is on line four."

"Okay, thank you, Denise. Please put him through."

"Will do."

"Mr. Valentine, good evening. What can I do for you?"

"Hello, Mona. How are you?"

"I'm well. Thanks for asking, but I would like to keep things between us professional. I prefer that you call me Ms. Cartwright."

"Would you like to know what I prefer?" Carter's sexy, deep voice said over the phone line.

Instantly, Mona's panties became very damp. Lately, she had been having similar reactions to Carter ever since he left her office, but compared to the steamy dreams that had been keeping her up all night, she welcomed this PG-13 moment.

"Mona?"

"Yes?"

"Would you like to know how I prefer you?"

"I'm sorry, but I don't think I heard you correctly."

Her heavy breathing had become very noticeable.

"Mona, you heard me just fine, but we can let it go for now. I was just calling to check on you, to make sure you were still doing okay and see if you needed anything."

"I-I'm alright. Thanks for being so concerned."

"Are you telling me the truth?"

"What reason would I have to lie to you?"

"I could think of quite a few, but I wouldn't want to embarrass you. However, I think it would only be fair since your flustered undertones and labored breathing is damn close to making me embarrass myself."

Mona didn't know what it was, but this man caused her body to react in ways it never had before. At that very moment, she swore he could hear her throbbing clit over the phone.

"Well, I'm telling you the truth, and I really have to get back to work."

"I guess I have to let you go then, but if I find out you've lied to me, all that labored breathing isn't going to be so labored anymore."

Oh my God, what in the hell is this man doing to me?

A few moments passed before she was finally able to respond. "I don't have time for this, Mr. Valentine."

"Are we still on for dinner next Saturday night?"

"Mr. Valentine, I don't know what kind of women you're used to dealing with, but when I say I'm going to do something, I do it."

"Good. So do I. And you better be sure to remember that. See you next week, beautiful."

Before she could respond, Carter had ended the call.

Tossing her phone to the side, Mona glanced back at her new centerpiece and then down at the card on the floor and shook her head. Why now? Mona stood and smelled the bouquet. She smiled at the memories of the many times Shaun would surprise her with a single rose just because.

With tears in her eyes, Mona carefully picked up the vase, hurled it across the room as hard as she could, and watched as the vase crashed into the wall and shattered. Pieces of glass, puddles of water, and broken flowers now littered her lounger and the carpet around it. She then exhaled, grabbed her phone, and exited her office as if nothing ever happened. While walking down the hall toward the lobby, Denise, one of the evening receptionists, and Monica, one of masseuses, rushed around the corner toward her.

"Oh my God! Are you okay?"

"Yeah, and what in the hell was that loud crash we heard?" Both women were frantic.

"Ladies, calm down. Everything is fine. I was just taking out the trash."

Chapter Four

Carter slowly sat up in his king-size bed and searched through the darkness until the blue neon numbers of his alarm clock came into view. Only two hours had passed since the last time he checked. Leaning over to the occupied space next to him, he watched as his latest conquest, Megan, slept soundlessly.

Damn, this woman is fine as hell, but she ain't got nothing on Mona. Where in the hell did that come from? Carter wondered as he paused the intimate act of tucking a few strands of her hair behind her ear.

Hell, who am I kidding? This is why I haven't been able to sleep since the day I walked into her business and royally pissed her off.

He frowned as he turned over on his back and placed his hands behind his head. His thoughts had been so consumed with Mona that he wasn't able to enjoy Megan like he'd planned. It took him a month of letting Megan think she had the upper hand, but he finally seduced her right into his bed. He had thought about keeping her around for a while and seriously exploring if something genuine was there, but all that flew out the window the minute he'd seen Mona. He felt a physical attraction so strong to her that he was a bit taken aback, as he'd never experienced these kinds of feelings before. From her brown eyes to her full lips and thick thighs, he wanted Mona bad. However, his business deal was standing in the way, and it was really starting to get under his skin.

Never before had he put pleasure before business, especially business with a contact that could really put his business on the map. Everyone in the real estate world wanted to work with Hollister Gram, but he was one of those big wigs who only worked with a select few. Gram owned several flawlessly-designed celebrity complexes in all of the big states and was known for personal, one-of-a-kind touches in his properties. So, when Gram called Carter's firm personally and told him that he wanted the building on the corner of Woodward and Grand River in downtown Detroit, and expressed he didn't care what dollar amount the owner wanted for him to acquire the property, Carter almost broke his neck jumping over his desk to get to the building and do his research. Once he got all his ducks in a row, he was ready to get Gram what he wanted. That is until he saw Mona and discovered she was the owner. He had to come up with a whole new game plan then. One that he still had yet to gather due to his mind-blowing attraction to her.

Throwing the cover back from over his body, he stood, took a deep breath, and stretched before heading for his study. After closing the door behind him, he sat and powered up his computer. While typing the words Soothing Touch Massage Spa into his search engine, he wondered what Mona was doing at that very moment.

He began reading the company's history and then opened his notes on her, wondering if there was anything he was missing. Carter had done thorough checks on Mona and her company, and nothing illegal or negative came up in her files. Mona Cartwright was actually running a legitimate business, which pissed Carter off because he had nothing to negotiate with her to get her to vacate the property. On one hand, part of him was elated she had no secrets when it came to her company, but he knew everyone had skeletons they didn't want dug up. He just had to search deeper to find them. Once found, he would then have to decide if he would use them against her or let them stay buried.

****

Shaun had just returned home from his morning jog and stepped into the shower, when a flashback of Mona pinned between him and the shower wall right before he slid between her thighs had suddenly caught him off guard. The memory was so strong that he had to brace himself against the towel bar behind him. Lately, his thoughts relentlessly consisted of Mona and their relationship. He hated to admit it, but he knew his thoughts were preoccupied with Mona because of how he did her when he ended their relationship. Shaun wondered if Mona had smiled when she learned the flowers were from him, or if she immediately slam-dunked them into the closest trash can.

He knew he deserved the latter, but he hoped...no, actually he prayed for the smallest smile. He'd regretted calling it quits the second he sent the text, but his father had strongly advised him that settling down in his early thirties would be the biggest mistake of his life and that Mona wasn't the type of woman you marry, only have fun with. So, against his better judgment, he took his father's advice and moved on, until the night he visited his quickly deteriorating grandmother. Shaun remembered the night like it was yesterday. The last thing his grandmother said to him was, "Instead of mourning my declining health, go get Mona back before it's too late." She told him that she loved him, and then she was gone.

He fought it at first because the loss of his grandmother had consumed him. However, once he began to really focus on what she said, he set in motion a plan to get his woman back, and he wasn't giving up until he held Mona in his arms again.

****

Mona walked into Red Lobster and was met by a grinning Carter who stood as she approached.

"You look amazing," Carter said.

He drank in her beauty as his eyes traveled from head to toe. Dressed in a green thigh-length dress, light gold blazer, and black rhinestone studded shades, she looked like an international supermodel.

"Thank you. You don't look so bad yourself," Mona replied, trying to hide her undeniable attraction to Carter as he stood in front of her in a grey button-up shirt, black jeans, and Rockports.

"Hi. Carter, party for two, right this way," the hostess said as she led them to their seat. "Here you are. Your server will be right with you."

"So," Carter began after the server took their order and left them alone, "How are you feeling?"

"I'm a little sore. Other than that, I'm okay. What about you?"

"Oh, I'm cool."

"Good. I...I was worried about you."

"Awww, ain't that cute," Carter teased.
"Forget I even said anything. You're such a jerk."

"Naw, seriously, I appreciate your concern, but I'm good. Really,

I am," Carter said, locking Mona in an intense stare.

He got a hard-on just looking at her. He needed to find something to silence his sexual tension quick.

"So, why out of all the restaurants you could've chosen, did you end up deciding on Red Lobster? I just knew we would end up at some upscale restaurant where the entrees were no less than a hundred dollars."

"Guess you just learned not to judge a book by its cover," Mona responded.

"I guess I have."

"Now, I have a question for you. Why did you only want dinner when I wrecked your Jag? What's your angle, Valentine?"

"Honestly, you intrigue me more than any other woman that has crossed my path in my 34 years of life. You're strong, smart, sassy, and very, very sexy. I won't lie. I've developed a very strong sexual attraction to you. And I don't believe I'm seriously about to admit this, but I haven't masturbated since I was 12. However, since that day in your office, I've gotten reacquainted with myself rather intimately, with images of you fueling my fantasies. There's also the fact that whether I like it or not, I am allowing you to come in between me doing my job. If I don't get you to accept my client's offer, I could lose millions. So, I invited you to dinner to pick your brain and see if you're worth me losing out on this huge account...and again millions. No woman on God's green earth has ever made me question millions."

Carter pinned Mona with another intense stare.

"So, I ask you, what is it that you think I should do?"

Mona was pissed because her nipples were straining through her dress, begging to be sucked. Her panties were wet and her clit was throbbing. She was angry Carter would stoop so low as to use her as a pawn to sabotage her business. She was hurt, sad, and confused.

"I...I...I have to go," Mona said, then jumped up and ran out of the restaurant.

"Women...they want honesty, but can't handle the truth." Carter shook his head in frustration.

.

Chapter Five

Mona was so deep in thought at her desk that the buzzing of the intercom system startled her.

"Ms. Cartwright?"

"Yes, Jamye?"

"A Mr. Valentine is here to see you."

Instantly, Mona pressed her thighs together and her clit began to throb uncontrollably. She hadn't had a decent night's sleep since she ran out during their date two weeks ago.

What in the hell is it about this man that has my body responding to him like this?

"Hello, Ms. Cartwright?"

"Huh? Oh, tell him now is not a good time. I'm on my way out."

After clicking off the intercom, Mona jumped up from her desk, grabbed her purse and briefcase, and headed for her office door. As soon as she turned the doorknob, she came face to face with Carter, who stood just outside the doorframe dressed in a very flattering black Armani suit and wearing the sexiest, sneakiest grin she'd ever seen.

"Hello, beautiful," Carter said as he grabbed Mona up by her waist, kicked the door closed behind him, and pinned her against the wall.

He slipped his hands underneath her blouse until he found her hardened nipples, which were eager for attention as he tweaked them while grinding his stiff cock into her slick wetness. Immediately, his lips went in search of hers, and he didn't stop his erotic assault until her lips were kiss swollen. Before letting Mona up for air, he made sure she had been thoroughly kissed.

"You think you're just going to dodge me after you turn my life upside down and I'll just go away?" Carter asked, his deep baritone voice low and seductive as he whispered into Mona's ear. His hands continued to roam the contours of her soft breasts.
"I...I...Carter this––"

"I have to get to work, but we will discuss this later on tonight. Understood?"

"I don't know if that's a good idea, Carter. We shouldn't even––"

Carter shoved Mona's thong panties to the side and slipped two fingers into her sweet nectar and a pebbled nipple into his mouth before Mona could finish her thought.

"Ohhh, Carter," Mona moaned as her hands cradled his head.

Her eyelids quickly closed as she savored the feeling of ecstasy. While shifting to caress Mona's other breast with the same addictive tongue-lashing, Carter guided his fingers deep and began increasing the speed of a third finger across her clit. Unable to take the sensitive feeling of passion any longer, she came all over his hand.

"Understood, Mona?"

"Y-yes."

"Good." Carter grinned as he licked her essence from his fingers.

"Have a great day, beautiful," he said, then released her and opened the door. "And, Mona, if I have to come looking for you, you're going to pay when I find you."

And with that, Carter was gone.

As her heartbeat slowly returned to its normal pace, Mona stood against the wall in shock at what just happened. She didn't know exactly when her nonexistent personal life spiraled out of control, but she had to get a hold of herself and quick. Only she was enjoying the spontaneity of what Carter brought into her humdrum life. Before the day he walked into her life, Mona was predictable and thought of nothing else but Soothing Touch. In such a short amount of time, though, Carter had her wondering what it would be like to stop and smell the roses for once.

Frustrated that her business was not her main priority and that her clit was still pounding, Mona headed for her shower to the left of her office door. She tried to wash away everything that had happened since Carter first entered her life.

A few hours later, Mona had mentally pulled herself together and not a moment too soon, because as soon as she stepped foot outside of her office door, she found her parlor bustling with business. Long lines of patrons were everywhere, the phones were ringing off the hook, the grey, silver, and black lobby was packed, and all 12 of the massage rooms were occupied. Immediately, Mona sprung into action, doing any and everything that needed her attention, and ended up working right through lunch and dinner. By the time she was able to take her first break of the day, it was one hour before closing time. Quickly, Mona returned to her office, jumped in the shower, slipped into a fitted white dress, and pinned up her long, flowing, curly black hair. While manning the phones earlier, Mona managed to place a call to her cousin and best friend Trina to meet up for drinks later to get some things off her chest.

Mona had just finished her makeup, when Courtney, her night manager, let her know she was going home. After walking Courtney to the door and watching as she got in her car, Mona poked her head in Sidney's room to let her know she was getting ready to go. Mona had just locked the door when a knock sounded at the main door. Ignoring it, Mona ran to retrieve her purse and jacket, then hightailed for the back door just in case it was Carter. She couldn't take another encounter with him anytime soon. She had made it to the back door and went to fish her keys out of her purse, when she remembered she'd sat them down on the service counter when she walked Courtney outside.

"Shit, shit, shit. You have got to be fucking kidding me," Mona whispered to herself.

After a few contemplating moments, Mona walked as fast as she could to the lobby in her stilettos. She made it to the lobby in record time, grabbed her keys from the desk, turned around, and almost ran right into her masseuse, Sidney, and her client as they were heading for the front door.

"Oh my God, I'm sorry," Mona apologized to Sidney's client.

"No worries." Her client smiled.

"Oh great, Mona, you're still here. I need to speak to you about something," Sidney said as she unlocked the door for her client.

"Oh, uh, let's chat about it in the morning," Mona replied, her eyes darting back and forth between the door and her exit.

"Well, it'll only take a moment. I promise," she said as she pulled the door closed.

When she saw the door close, her tense body visibly calmed.

"Okay, shoot."

"Well, I was—Oh, just a second. Someone's at the door."

"Hi. I'm sorry, but we're closed."

"I know. Mona's expecting me," Carter stated from the other side of the entrance to the parlor.

"Oh, okay. Just a minute. Mona, someone's––"

"It's fine. Let him in."

As soon as Carter stepped inside, Mona knew that he knew she had been trying to sneak away. And the way his eyes traveled her body and the way her body responded, her night was far from over.

"You know, on second thought, I'll just talk to you in the morning." Sidney smiled, grabbed her things from her room, and headed out the back door.

.

.

Chapter Six

"Did you seriously think--"

"Look, Carter, I can't deal with this right now. It's late. I need to clear my head and my cousin is waiting for me."

"Okay, I'll go."

"Thank you."

"If you give me a massage."

"What? No. I'm exhausted," Mona whined.

"Come on, one massage," Carter said as he locked the front door and headed straight for Mona.

Mona could see Carter wasn't going to go away until she gave in. So, she did.

"Fine, Carter. One massage, and that's it. Go into the first room to your left."

Mona sat her things down and then walked off toward the supply closet down the hall. Grabbing what she needed, she headed back to the paradise room, but Carter was nowhere to be found.

"Carter, where are you?"

"In here."

"Well, come in here. You're in the wrong room."

Mona had set up everything she needed, but there was still no sign of Carter.

"Carter, come--"

"I'd rather be in this room," came his deep voice from across the hall.

The soft glow coming from the room had caught Carter's attention while standing in the hall. Feeding his curiosity, he pushed open the room and walked inside. The small room, housed between four deep red walls adorned with lipstick prints and erotic art of couple in various sex positions, immediately piqued his interest. The room emulated sexual tension and seduced him as he walked further inside. Assorted candles covered every surface and rose petals were sprinkled across the massage table. A burnt orange waterfall sat behind the workstation and next to a bamboo supply closet, while the sweet smell of warming brown sugar added the final touch to the red room. A huge stereo sat atop the burnt orange corner counter.

"Carter, this room is for couples only," Mona told him, while leaning against the doorframe.

"So?"

"What part of couples don't you understand?"

Ignoring her, Carter asked, "What's this room called by the way?"

"The Red Room."

"The Red Room, huh? Why? Because the color red implies a sensual offering, and the room was designed specifically for couples looking to heighten their passion, so when they leave here, they immediately desire to please one another for hours on end. If so, I'll take my massage in here, please."

Carter flashed his kilowatt smile, and instantly, wetness began to pool in her panties.

"Anybody ever tell you what an enormous jerk you are?" Mona asked, trying to curb her quickly growing attraction to this man.

"As a matter of fact, many times, but we can discuss that later. Come on over here, sexy, and calm my body," Carter said as he began removing his suit jacket.

He held Mona in a very tense sexual stare before she quickly severed contact and began setting up for the massage.

"Okay, Carter, here's the deal. You get a 15-minute massage and then you––"

Sweet Jesus!

When Mona turned around, the last thing she expected to see was Carter completely nude and his long, thick dick saluting her.

"And then what, Mona?" Carter asked as if standing there naked was the most normal thing in the world.

"Uh-uh-nothing. Just get on the table and cover up with the sheet, please. I'll be right back."

Mona ran down the hall to her office, locked the door, scurried across the room to her desk drawer, and pulled out her vibrator. Kicking off her heels, she sat in her chair, spread her legs on her desk, and slowly eased her rabbit pearl vibrator in between her soaked pussy lips.

"Oh, yesss. Oh, Carter," she moaned softly.

Her head fell back into the headrest and ecstasy began to curl her toes. Being so horny, it didn't take long before a big orgasm tore through her body as she fingered her clit and grinded her honey pot against the vibrator.

"Ohhhh...shit, yes," Mona moaned, the aftershocks of the orgasm continuing to torment her body.

As soon as her orgasm subsided, she jumped up, washed off her toy, and headed back to the Red Room confident that she could deal with Carter better now that she wasn't horny anymore.

"Okay, you ready?" Mona asked as she walked into the room, grabbed her work smock and oils, and wheeled the small cart to the side of the table.

"Are you ready?" Carter shot back.

Does he know what I just did? Naw, he couldn't.

Shaking off the thought, Mona said, "I sure am."

After she turned the radio on smooth jazz V98.7, she grabbed the oil, drizzled it on his back, and began to work it into his soft, smooth brown skin. As Mona worked the oil into his toned arms, muscular back, and chiseled sides, her clit began to pulse with need. She was somehow hornier now than she was when she'd seen his huge cock. Just thinking about Carter's dick had her biting her bottom lip to keep from moaning as she continued to work his upper body.

I can't do this shit anymore. I have to get this man out of here right now.

"Okay, Carter, time's up. You--"

"I thought that 15 minutes would never pass. Come here."

Carter sat up, pulled the blanket off his body, exposing his solid cock, and pulled Mona into his strong arms and legs in one swift motion. Before Mona could contest, Carter's lips were on hers, and his tongue explored her mouth with purpose and need. His hands followed suit as they palmed the curves of her thick hips and thighs, saving her ass for a two-handed squeeze.

"Carter, we-we can't do this," Mona sputtered between breathless kisses, while Carter sucked her bottom lip and pulled her short dress up, revealing her lace-covered cheeks.

"Why can't we?" he asked as his kisses began to travel toward her ample breasts.

"'Cause it's not right, Carter. This is too soon."

"I think your lips strongly disagree."

Mona's juices seeped out onto his fingers before he actually slid them inside her flowing warmth. The second the wetness blanketed his fingers, his eyes closed and he hissed out in need. He was driving himself delirious with lust and craving her sweet smelling sex.

"Fuck, Mona, I got to taste you now."

.

.

Chapter Seven

Carter grabbed her up, laid her on the table, ripped her dress and smock, and watched as it tore a path to the last strand of thread before collapsing at her side. Pulling her ass to the edge, he knelt down and slipped his tongue deep inside of Mona. At first taste, he was addicted and knew he would be feasting for a while. So, he paused long enough to grab the stepstool, quickly placing it beneath him, and slowly slipped his tongue back in between Mona's trembling thighs. With Mona's thighs spread wide and resting on his shoulders, Carter went deep and took his sweet time savoring every lick of her delicious center. Since he began, he had purposely avoided Mona's clit, focusing only on sucking her fat lips and swirling his tongue deep inside the drenched walls of her pussy to torture her. He enjoyed every minute of it as she thrust her throbbing clit toward his mouth. He brushed across it with his tongue to torment her even more.

"Please, Carter. Fuck...please..." Mona begged as she thrashed about on the table so close to orgasm, yet so far away.

"Please what, Mona?" Carter asked as he continued his torment in, around, and through her thick honey.

She tasted so good that his addiction was growing by leaps and bounds. He wanted to make her pay for making him this horny, this out of control, since the day he first walked into her office. No woman had ever made him feel this far gone just by tasting her. His dick concrete, he began to stroke himself with one hand while holding her thigh immobile with his other hand. He sped up his slow tongue strokes to match Mona's more pointed speed. He flattened his tongue, then spun circles deep into Mona's dripping desire before finally sliding her engorged clit into his mouth. As soon as he closed his mouth around the slippery wet nub and softly bit the slick flesh, Mona squirted all over his face.

"Ahhhh, fuck!" Mona yelled, her orgasm shaking her to the core.

Carter was almost chin deep in Mona's pussy, lapping up as much of her essence as he could before finally succumbing to his own hefty nut.

"Ohhh shit!" he yelled as cum squirted all over his hand and the massage table.

As Carter's orgasm began to subside, his dick slowly lost its hardness. He laid his head on Mona's thigh, and as soon as her sweet smell filled his nasal cavity, his dick jerked, and just like that, he was hard all over again. Quickly, Carter stood and began backing away from a still slightly shaking Mona, as aftershocks continued to run rampant through her body. Spotting his clothes, he quickly dressed before walking over to Mona, helping her sit upright.

"Sorry about your dress. I'll send you a new one," Carter told her.

He took in her bed head, ripped clothes, sticky thighs, and how sexy she was even when she wasn't trying to be. He wanted so badly to fuck her on the table he was leaning against, but he didn't want his first time with her to be rushed.

41

"That's okay, Carter. You don't have to do that." Mona ran a hand through her mane and smiled.

"Listen, I need to sort this shit out with my job before we――"

"Carter, I understand. You don't owe me any explanations. I stake no claim over you," she said as she hopped down from the table and made her way to the door. "I'm a big girl and was well aware of what we were doing. I need to go get myself cleaned up. Let yourself out, will you?"

"Mona――"

"Goodnight, Carter," Mona said before gently shutting the door behind her.

Mona hadn't placed both feet into the shower before she began wondering again if she had been set up. She knew Carter still wanted to buy her out, but she wasn't sure just how low he'd go to get his hands on her parlor. Immediately, tears began to cloud her vision. She felt used and ashamed, even though they technically didn't have sex. So caught up in how he made her feel, she had unknowingly let her guard down again. Yeah, he had been upfront about wanting to close down her parlor, but in the midst of the blazing chemistry between them, the thought of him doing whatever it took to secure that account had totally slipped her mind.

Soothing Touch meant everything to her, and for the first time in years, she slowly felt it slipping away. Mona still didn't have any proof to support all of the crazy thoughts in her head, so she decided to just let the matter go for now and finally head home.

After gathering all of her personal belongings, Mona double-checked all of the rooms before quickly prepping the Red Room for the masseuses the next day. While stripping the massage table of the soiled linen, a beeping sound cut into her flashbacks with Carter. At first, she thought it was the radio, but as soon as she pressed the power button to turn it off, she heard it again. Following the direction of the noise over by the closet, Mona pushed the door closed and found what she thought was a cell phone on the floor. Upon closer inspection, she learned it wasn't a cell phone at all. It was a mini camcorder.

Mona's whole body froze as soon as she hit the play button. What had just made her feel so good only a few hours ago now had her sick to her stomach. Mona knew something wasn't right with the way Carter was acting after their interlude. Now she had her proof. Carter Valentine was trying to blackmail her and run her business into the ground. Looking around the Red Room, an idea made Mona grin deviously.

"Okay, Mr. Valentine, it's about time I teach you a lesson you'll never forget," Mona said just as the camcorder battery popped up, turned red, and the whole screen went black.

****

"How close are you to acquiring my property, Mr. Alexander?" Hollister asked before placing the Styrofoam cup to his thin lips. He gingerly sipped his hot coffee and took in his surroundings while waiting on Carter to respond.

Clearing his throat, Carter waited until the waitress dropped off his coffee and left before he replied, "We are still in negations at the moment."

Deciding to meet up at Elise's Donuts, the two were now occupying the corner booth in the back of the bakery.

"And how much longer do you expect us to be in limbo? You do understand my time is very precious and I only deal with the best. I was told you were the best and your track record speaks for itself. So, there was no doubt in my decision to retain your services. I have no reason to doubt my decision, do I?"

"Not at all. Wrapping up is just taking a bit longer than normal due to a stubborn tenant."

"But you specialize in stubborn--"

"I do, and I will get this property. I just have to work this one from a different angle. There is no need for you to worry. You will be able to start your project on time," Carter stated, while trying to hide his quickly growing annoyance at the direction their conversation was headed.

"I don't worry, Mr. Alexander. I cause other people to worry. I am concerned, however, that once this parlor goes under, the state will get a hold of the property. And while I have no doubt that I will meet their ridiculous price, dealing with them comes with a whole set of issues I'd rather avoid."

"As I've said, Gram, everything is already taken care of. Should a situation I can't handle arise, you will be the first to know," Carter finished as he bit into his donut.

"How much longer do you anticipate the job will take?"

"Two weeks tops."

"You have exactly two weeks to get my property, or I will find another agency, and then sue you for wasting my time."

"I don't take too kindly to threats, Gram. Now, if you'll excuse me, I have better things to do with my time."

"Alexander, that wasn't a threat."

.

.

Chapter Eight

Still seething from discovering that Carter had actually intended to blackmail her, work had been the furthest thing from Mona's mind. She still hadn't decided on a plan for how to deal with the situation. Since she couldn't focus and only managed to give herself a horrible headache, she shut down her computer and left work early for the first time in six years, and that time was only because her great aunt Marjorie died.

Grabbing her purse, Mona turned off the light and headed for her white 2012 Buick Lacross. As soon as she stepped out in the humid afternoon, the smell of fresh donuts from Elise's caused her mouth to water immediately. Quickly sliding behind the wheel, Mona started the engine, shifted her car in reverse, and hightailed it across the street to the first parking space available. Walking into the bakery, Mona stood in line and smiled as she watched the waiter slide a tray of fresh-baked large cinnamon rolls into the display case.

"Finally, a woman after my own heart," the man behind her laughed.

"Excuse me?" Mona turned slightly toward the voice. She could barely tear her eyes away from all the delicious looking desserts.

"I see you have a cinnamon roll addiction, as well." He smiled and pointed to the case.

"Oh, yeah. Mine is so bad that my jeans and I aren't speaking at the moment." Mona smiled back.

"How about we talk about co-hosting a donuts anonymous group over dinner sometime, beautiful?"

"Oh uh, I'm sorry, but I'm not dating at the moment."

"But you do still eat, right?"

"On occasion," she laughed.

"Well, how about we discuss that group here instead? I mean, what better place to gather all the cons of these delicious little pastries? And over freshly glazed cinnamon rolls, of course."

"Oh, of course." She smiled.

"So, what do you say? I'll even throw in a Frappuccino. If I were a betting man, I'd say you're an iced coffee kind of lady."

"Too bad you're not a betting man, because you could've hit big. Maybe you should take up gambling."

"I'll be sure to keep that in mind. So, how about that date?"

"Mona."

"I'm sorry?"

"My name is Mona."

"Hollister, Hollister Gram." He extended his hand.

"Nice to meet you, Hollister." Mona smiled as she placed her hand in his.

"Likewise, pretty lady. Do we have a date, Mona?"

"How bad do you want that date, Hollister?"

"Woman, with you, damn bad."

"Good answer. It's a date. Meet me here next Thursday evening at seven. Bye."

"Wait. Don't we need to exchange numbers? How do I know you won't stand me up?"

"You don't. Guess you'll just have to wait until next week to find out. Enjoy the rest of your evening, Hollister."

****

Carter sat on the concrete steps of his back porch, raised the red plastic cup of Remy on the rocks to his lips, and took another sip. He'd been posted in that same spot for the last hour and a half wondering what in the hell was happening to him. He couldn't believe he was actually letting a woman come in between him and his livelihood. Nor could he believe he'd left the same woman in a room with her legs spread eagle and her body still shaking from the aftershocks of a soul-shaking orgasm. Carter's dick instantly pressed against the thin material of his boxers and tried to bust through his jeans. Adjusting himself as best he could, he took another swig of Remy and began to map out his next move. An hour later, he was hard as a brick and had accomplished nothing. Even more frustrated than when he'd first come outside, he headed back inside his house and went into the kitchen to grab his jacket.

Maybe once I watch this tape and bust this nut, I'll be able to focus.

Reaching into the hidden pocket on the inside of his jacket, he felt around for the small camcorder that he planted at Mona's as soon as she'd left him alone in the Red Room. When he felt nothing but lint in his pocket, he quickly snatched his jacket up from hanging on the back of the kitchen chair. His heart began racing as he checked the other two, calming only when he felt the long, thin object. However, after pulling it out, he discovered it was his cell phone. Dropping his phone on the table, he went into full panic mode as he checked his pockets again but came up empty again. Carter threw his jacket, ran to the front door, grabbed his briefcase, popped it open, and tore through all the contents. Still nothing.

Not yet ready to face facts, Carter started searching from the cushions of his sectional in the living room and didn't stop until he reached the trunk of his Jaguar in the garage. Heaving with anger, he slammed his trunk shut, leaned up against it, and ran his hands down his face.

"Gotdamn it!"

Only then did he finally allow reality to set in. Only then did he finally accept the fact that the camcorder must've fallen out of his pocket in his haste to get away from Mona as quickly as he could.

"Shit!"

As he walked back through his side door, Carter remembered the battery on the recorder was low.

"Fuck! I hope the batteries died. I hope Mona didn't find that fucking camcorder!"

Guess there's only one way to find out.

****

Mona sat in the middle of her queen-size bed propped up on her leopard body pillows, eyeing the camcorder and pack of batteries she stopped to pick up on her way home. She was so angry the first couple of days after finding the recorder that she'd contemplated destroying the tape and mailing the beat-up camera back to Carter, but curiosity got the best of her. She needed to know just how much of this movie she starred in and what else, if anything, was on the tape. Ripping open the pack of new batteries, Mona replaced them with the old ones, waited a few minutes, and then hit the play button. Immediately, the Red Room came into focus, showing when she began massaging Carter's body. Not much longer after that, Carter's lips had found the wet lips between her thighs and began French kissing her very essence.

Instead of being pissed off like she had been, she became extremely aroused watching herself on camera. Between reliving the moment and hearing herself moaning, Mona grew so horny that she slipped one hand beneath her black comforter and between her thighs. She didn't stop until she sought out her slippery wet heat. Immediately, she found a succulent stroke that had her moaning almost as loud as she was on camera. Mona's body hummed with orgasmic sensations as she relived the vibrations and movement of Carter's tongue as he made love to her pussy. As Mona watched and listened to Carter bring her to ecstasy, her entire body shook and responded to him as if his head was between her trembling thighs at that moment. Leaning over her bed, Mona reached into her nightstand, grabbed her G-spot vibrator, and pressed the power button.

Switching the camcorder to her left hand, she tossed back the covers and slid the soft, curved vibrator inside her drenched wetness. When the vibrations hit her, her eyes immediately closed, and she could feel the camera slowly slipping from her grasp. Looking around her bedroom for something to sit the camera on so she could cum while watching herself cum, Mona spotted a shoebox and was about to get up to get it, when she remembered pillows surrounded her. Grabbing the one she rubbed against her clit many nights and affectionately called Kevin, Mona pulled it beneath her legs, propped the camcorder on it, and began sliding the vibrator in and out of her wet pussy. Raising her left hand to tweak her hardened nipples, she could feel her body begging for release as she watched Carter spread her legs wider and go deeper.

Remembering that night and watching them together was such an erotic experience that it wasn't long before she could almost feel Carter's tongue and lips replace the toy. They were back in the Red Room, and she could feel every single push, pull, and curl of his tongue. That coupled with her moans on and off screen, and the sight of her and Carter, was all it took for Mona to squirt all over the covers and camcorder.

"Ohhh yessss, Carterrr! Fuck!"

Once Mona's heart rate returned to normal, she grinned from ear to ear.

"Slight change of plans, Mr. Valentine. Your blackmailing days are over. But mine have just begun."

Chapter Nine

Hollister strolled into Elise's Bakery and ordered his usual: a large coffee and a freshly baked cinnamon roll. He walked over to the only available booth with a view of the early evening traffic making its way down Grand River in a light drizzling rain. As he bit into his warm, soft, and slightly sticky pastry, he wondered if Mona had any real intention of showing up. Hollister hadn't been able to get the intriguing beauty out of his mind all week long and was looking forward to seeing Mona more then he cared to admit. He didn't usually involve himself in getting to know anything about a woman he was attracted to other than what her favorite position was and how fast he could get her there. But with Mona, he actually couldn't wait to learn more about her. He couldn't wait for her amazing smile and classic, yet one of a kind beauty to light up his world. Her thick size 14 frame, her memorizing dark brown—almost black eyes, perfect pouty lips, and long curly mane had him up all night—and in more ways than one. The thought of running his fingers across her smooth peanut butter-hued skin practically drove him wild.

Glancing down at his wrist watch, he noticed that he'd been there for almost an hour and was still alone. He signed heavily, glancing at the empty pastry wrapper, before looking more closely at the passing women who scurried by the storefront, running from the rain.

There was still no sign of her.

After another 20 minutes passed, Hollister had concluded that he'd been stood up. He downed the remainder of his lukewarm coffee, dropped a five dollar bill on the table, and made his way to the exit. Just as soon as he tossed his empty cup into the trash and turned to open the door, there was Mona running across the parking lot trying to dodge puddles of rainwater. In all his sulking, he hadn't noticed the rainfall was pretty heavy. When she finally made it to the door, the sight of her up close almost knocked the wind out of him.

"Thank you," Mona said as she hurried by him out of the rain. She shivered and closed her red umbrella. He took her entire outfit into view—the tight fitted red dress and red and black pumps.

Damn! This woman is—Damn!

Hollister locked eyes with her and for a minute, they both just stood there, casually taking each other in. Both of their lingering stares seemed to challenge the other to see who would look away first. Surprisingly, Hollister was the first to clear his throat and glanced in the other direction, toward his empty booth with a street view.

"Wow Mona, you look amazing."

"Thank you. You weren't leaving, were you Hollister? Because if so, I'll just go and—"

"No, I was j—just uh…going t-to grab another coffee. Can I get you anything?" he stuttered while making his way to the service counter.

What the hell? I haven't stuttered since I was 14.

"Yes, please. I'll have a caramel Frappuccino with extra caramel and a cinnamon roll."

"Okay, no problem."

"Thank you." Mona sashayed over to the booth that Hollister had just vacated and slid across the worn tan seat.

Lord have mercy, this man is talk-your-panties-off fine. With his special-edition dark chocolate skin, dimpled smile, and sexy bald head...mmmmmm... But these fine ones always come with some kind of hang-up. I wonder what his issue is. But hey, at least he's not trying to take over my business or blackmail me like Carter's intolerable ass did.

As she waited for Hollister to deliver the goods, Mona's thoughts drifted back to Carter and she couldn't help but squeeze her thighs together. There was something about that incorrigible man that drove her wild with sexual desire and something else that she couldn't quite put her finger on. And she was almost tempted to explore that something else; until she found out that he was trying to blackmail her to take over her business.

What a jerk! I've never hated someone so much in my entire life. She sighed at the thought of his schemes. *But Carter is going to pay for trying to ruin my life and whoever he's working for is going to pay, too.*

"Okay, here you are, beautiful." Hollister placed the fresh pastry and iced coffee in front of her.

"So, judging from the looks of things when I first walked in, you didn't think I'd show, huh?"

"Nah, I just figured that you were just running late or something."

"Oh, stop lying," she laughed.

"Alright, you got me. I wasn't sure, but I thought you stood me up," he chuckled.

"If nothing else, I'm a woman of my word. The weather just got worse and worse."

"Well, I had no way of knowing that, Ms. Mona, and folks word rarely means anything nowadays."

"Yeah, you're right. Unfortunately, I know exactly what you mean. But on another note, what in the world do you know about Elise Donuts?"

"Me? I was going to ask you the same thing. You're the one that looks like you only buy your coffee and scones from those high end coffee shops, similar to the ones in Neman Marcus and Lord and Taylors."

"Ha! Really? *Scones?* Well, while I do shop in both of those stores, I can't stand the coffee from their specialty cafes. And I don't do scones at all. Do I really give that impression?"

"I think that's a trick question, but I'll answer it anyway. It's just the way you carry yourself. You appear to be a very no-nonsense, stuck-up lawyer, who thinks all men are dogs and both of your parents are either doctors, lawyers, or dentists. Matter fact, you're Gabrielle Union in that movie, Daddy's Little Girls." Mona laughed so hard she almost spit her coffee across the table.

"I take it you've heard that before?" Hollister grinned wide.

"Not to such a degree, but I get that all the time. I've been told that I give off a stuck up demeanor upon first impression. I'm nowhere near stuck up though, and the closest I've ever come to being a lawyer is watching Law and Order: Criminal Intent. I don't think all men are dogs, just *most* of them. But my dad *is* a doctor." Mona smiled. "I'm just surprised that *you* would say that though, with your whole high end, 'I only wear name brand suits' look. You wouldn't buy coffee from Starbucks on a bad day."

A sexy grin spread across his sexy lips. "I have never gotten *that* before and I can't stand Starbucks or any kind of specialty coffee. I'm just a city boy who loves city coffee."

"Well alright, city boy. I guess we both just reminded each other how important it is not to judge a book by its cover."

"I agree. And since I now know that you're not a lawyer, what is it that you do beautiful?"

"I'm a masseuse and owner of The Soothing Touch Massage Parlor. And I'm located right across the street. You should stop in sometime and let me show you what we can do."

" *You* are the owner of The Soothing Touch?"

"Yes, have you heard of us before?"

"Yes, actually. A friend was just suggesting that I pay your place a visit just last week."

"Really?"

"Yes, and now I am definitely going to take his advice."

"Great. I can't wait to get you scheduled."

"Neither can I, beautiful. Neither can I."

****

Carter pulled into the Speedway gas station next to Elise's Donuts and parked his car on the opposite side of the building next to the air pump and cut the engine. Reaching across the leather seat of his Land Rover, he grabbed his IPhone and checked the time. He glanced across the street at the Soothing Touch. It was Thursday, and Carter knew that Mona closed early on Thursdays and left her night manager to tend to the closing duties. He called and spoke briefly with Mona this morning about grabbing a bite to eat so he could explain his actions from last week, but not once during the brief conversation did she say or allude to knowing anything about the recorder. But he knew just from the few encounters with her, that Mona was a very smart woman and only played her cards close to her chest. And that if she knew anything, she wasn't going to just give it up. So, he decided to return to the scene of the crime, hoping and praying that the recorder had fallen behind a piece of furniture in the Red Room, and that Mona knew nothing about it.

As he exited his car, the aroma of fresh donuts and coffee instantly made him turn his head and contemplate whether he should grab a donut before crossing the street to the parlor. It didn't take five seconds before Carter listened to his grumbling stomach and detoured to the bakery. As he rounded the walkway and made his way to the side entrance, the familiar view of a woman's slightly turned face caught his eye. Upon closer inspection, Carter immediately knew that it was Mona sitting at the window, even though the tree in front of the building was practically obstructing his view. Deciding to join her in hopes of getting a better feel for her demeanor in person, Carter hastened his pace to the entrance. He halted his footsteps almost immediately when he saw Hollister Gram slide in the booth across from her. Quickly, he backed up and ducked behind the tree. A million thoughts ran through his mind as he backtracked to his truck.

What the hell? How do they know each other? Maybe she does have the tape? Does Gram know? Just what in the hell is going on here?

Back at his vehicle, Carter contemplated his next move, with Mona so close to the parlor, he wasn't as confident about finding a way into the Red Room as he was on the drive over. Backing out from the side of the gas station, he felt that there was no need to hide his vehicle in case Mona drove because Mona was already pretty distracted already. Even though the man who was distracting her was royally pissing him off, he knew this would be his best chance to check. Driving around the corner, Carter pulled into the parlor parking lot from the alley, jumped out, and ran inside.

"Hello, welcome to the Soothing Touch, how may I help you today?" Jayme smiled.

"Yes, I have a card that I would like to give to Ms. Cartwright," Carter said as he pulled a red envelope from the inside of his breast pocket with Mona's name on it.

"I'm sorry, but she's not in at the moment, but feel free to leave it with me, if you'd like."

"It's a very pressing and personal matter. I'm not saying that you would open it, but do-- you would think that it would be alright if I could place it on her desk myself, or perhaps slide it under her door?"

"I'm sorry, but I can't let you go into Ms. Cartwright's office."

"Jayme," Carter read the fancy name tag pinned to her chest, "if your man wanted to surprise you—if he wanted to plan out every single detail on his own, would you really want someone to stop him from doing so, lovely lady?" Carter slid that sexy kilowatt smile in place and she was a goner.

She blushed. "Oh, go ahead. But please, make it quick."

"Thank you. Be back in a flash, pretty lady." He grinned at her and briskly took off down the hall. As he neared the partially open door, he looked both ways and went to slip inside when he noticed a purse and clothing laying across the bench by the door that wasn't there last week and heard soft giggles coming from behind the door.

"Shit." Carter quickly took off down the hall to the left and into the men's restroom.

"Damn!" Carter slammed his fists down on the sink and shook his head in frustration.

"Why in the hell didn't I think that the room could be occupied in the middle of the damn evening? Fuckin' stupid." He slammed his fist down on the sink again. "Fuck it. I'll just come back tomorrow."

Carter started back toward the lobby when the woman that he heard giggling and her partner came walking out of the Red Room followed by the masseuse. Before anyone could see him, Carter darted across the hall and hid in the opening of the Safari Oasis room and waited until their footsteps faded. As soon as the footsteps left the lobby, Carter ran across the hall and dashed into the room.

.

Chapter Ten

Carter began searching for the recorder immediately. He moved swiftly, he had to find that tape, and he had to do it before someone began to suspect he was up to something and come looking for him.

"*Please*, let it still be here."

He was quiet and careful as he moved every piece of furniture that wasn't nailed down. He had practically turned the entire room upside down and yet, still nothing. The only piece of furniture left to check behind was the old fashioned chest in the corner. Rushing toward it, he gathered all his strength and pulled the chest from the wall. Falling to his knees, he looked and felt around on the floor, but no such luck. Just when he was about to call it quits and face the music, his hands brushed across something hard as he pulled it from the back corner. Slowly, he slid his hand back across the hardwood floor underneath the chest and stopped as his hand grasped the hard square object as he pulled it out.

"Oh, thank God," he visibly sighed with relief.

Turning on the recorder, the red dangerously low light flashed once then powered off instantly.

"Yes." A smile now replaced his worry lines and apparent panic.

Carter was busy soaking in relief that by the time he stood, straightened and pushed everything back in its place and headed for the door, he heard new approaching footsteps. Nervous energy and slight panic filled him as his brain rapidly registered that it was too late to just ease out without going unnoticed.

As footsteps sounded closer, he desperately searched the room for a place to hide before he ended up knee deep in shit. Jetting across the room, he hid in the only place he could, just as he eased his large frame behind the bamboo closet and pulled it back toward him into its exact angle up against the wall, the door to the red room opened and the masseuse walked in yelling into her phone as she slammed the door behind her. Half an hour later, the oblivious woman had cleaned up and put the room back in order before finally exited the room, never realizing that the closet wasn't closed the first time she'd left.

"Damn! Finally! She lucky I wasn't hired to take her out. She never would've had a chance," Carter whispered as he slowly eased out from behind the closet and scurried toward the door. Placing his ear to the door, he listened for any hallway traffic. When the coast was clear, he turned the knob and slowly opened the door. Poking his head out, he looked both ways before easing out the door, softly pulling it closed behind him.

Carter took a deep breath and exhaled. He couldn't believe his luck, he was home free and Mona would never know about the tape unless he wanted her to. He was almost to the lobby when he felt someone behind him. Her alluring soft scent got to him first. Hit him like a glass of cold water on a hot summer morning. Then not two seconds later, he felt a tap on his shoulder.

"Carter, hey. What are you doing here?"

Jerking around, he came face to face with Mona smiling up at him and looking sexy as ever.

"H-hey, I was uh-just coming from the restroom. I came by to see if you wanted to join me for a late dinner."

"Oh okay, well if the offer still stands, I would love to join you."

"Absolutely, the offer still stands. Are you ready to head out now?"

"Actually, if you could give me about 15 minutes, I'll be ready. My manager had to leave immediately, right in the middle of closing for the evening due to a family emergency. So, I have to close up shop."

"Alright, I understand, take your time. I'll be waiting for you out front."

"Okay great." Mona smiled and headed toward her office.

Fifteen minutes later, Mona was knocking on his truck window.

"Carter, could you come back inside for a quick minute, I need help moving some furniture before we go."

"No problem," Carter said as he followed Mona back inside.

"I really appreciate this, Carter. I have been trying to get help moving this heavy old fashioned chest in the red room all week," she lied as he locked the front door behind them and crossed the lobby.

Carter froze in his tracks as Mona's words began to sink in. *Oh shit, she knows.*

"Carter, are you okay?" Mona raised a curious brow when she looked over her shoulder and noticed that Carter was still standing by the entrance.

How in the hell am I going to get out of this? His thoughts were racing a mile a minute. He had to think fast.

"Carter?"

"I'm sorry, what was that?"

"Is everything okay?"

"Yeah, everything is good. Let's get this chest moved so we can get to dinner." He smiled. *Fuck it, I'll think of something. Even if I end up having to tell her the truth.*

"You can go ahead inside, I have to grab something from my office. I'll be right back."

"Okay."

Mona scuttled ahead to her office while Carter slowly walked into the Red Room, unsure if an ambush awaited him on the other side of the door. Turning the knob, Carter pushed the door open and walked inside.

What the hell? A vast variety of vanilla scented candles, circled the length of the room. Rose petals covered the floor and littered the massage tables that had been pushed together and lined with a red silk sheet that now gave the appearance of an actual bed. Handcuffs and a blindfold hung from the chest door all while soft slow jam music serenaded the background. Carter couldn't believe that he was just in this room, not nearly 30 minutes ago. He didn't know what the hell was going on, but something didn't feel right. He began to back out of the room   while still trying to register the scene before him, when he backed into Mona standing in the doorway. Startled, he jumped as he spun around to face her.

"I thought we'd finished where we left off."

"Where we left— "

Before Carter could finish his sentence, Mona had already untied the belt on her plush, white robe, to reveal a blood red peek-a-boo teddy and matching red peek-a-boo pumps. He stood there gulping for air, his instant hard-on was straining for the visibly wet cleanly shaven 'V' of her thighs thanks to the missing patch of material.

"Listen, I think we need to—"

Mona crossed the room to him and gently placed her index finger on his lips and smiled. Next, she began to slowly undress him. She started with his shirt, taking her time undoing every button. Every once in a while she would glance up into his eyes, then finish the simple task that she was purposely dragging out as she moved her small hands down to his jeans and with a flick of the wrist, his pants were sliding down his sculpted legs.

Removing her robe, Mona hopped up on the massage table, resting on her elbows and spread her legs. With the perfect and elegant way she'd spread her legs apart and effortlessly held them up in the air, Carter could tell that Mona had some real experience in dance, gymnastics, or both. And that thought alone of what else she could do with her those gorgeous legs had him so hard, his dick began leading him by the balls toward the sweet nectar that she offered to him. While locking eyes with her, he parted her pussy lips with two fingers then slipped them inside her warm wetness.

Breathing deeply, he slowly slid his drenched fingers out, raised them to his lips and sucked them dry of Mona's essence. "Goddamn woman, you taste so sweet. And you so fucking wet."

"I get sweeter and wetter, too," she whispered to him. The erotic sight of her and her soft, sexy voice was all he needed to push him over the edge. He grabbed Mona's hips, and slipped right inside of her. As soon as her pussy smothered his nine inches, Mona wrapped her legs around Carter's waist and tried to pull him in even deeper. His initial plunge into her wetness captivated her, and as she cried out in the sweetest ecstasy, he filled her thoroughly, completely.

"Oh fuck. Yessss, oh yes."

Back and forth they moved, exchanging powerful thrusts all across the table.

"Got damn, woman, I could stay in you forever." Carter grunted when Mona unhooked her legs from around him and laid flat on her back. Pulling her into the center of the table, he drew her legs up to her shoulders and pummeled her sweet juicy pussy repeatedly. Reaching for her breasts as they followed his rhythmic thrusts, he pulled a nipple into his mouth and sucked tenderly and with just the right amount of pressure to see her eyes roll straight up.

Reaching for his waist, Mona dragged her nails across his back and tried to pull him in deeper still. "Ohhhhh. Fuck."

All Mona could do was scream and moan as Carter laid into her wet heat, hitting her g-spot until she couldn't take anymore.

"Carterrrrr!" she screamed and squirted all over his dick.

Carter didn't give her one moment of reprieve, before he pulled out, helped her to her knees, and slipped back inside from behind.

"Mona! Shitttt!" Carter exhaled as he slid back into her warm slippery opening. His hands instantly found her hips and plunged into her, each thrust more aggressive than the last.

"Yes, daddy. I'm cumming again. Ohhhhh yessss. Fuuuuckkk, yeeeesss!" Mona screamed as he deliciously continued to pound her from behind. She welcomed every single plunge as she bounced back onto Carter's dick until he was ready to explode.

And a few dozen strokes later, he did. "Ughhhhhh, fuck!" He hadn't cum so hard in a long time.

"Damn woman, your ass is phenomenal!" He kissed her ass cheek before collapsing next to her. When he tried to go in for a kiss, Mona dodged his sexy lips effortlessly. Sitting up, she looked around the room for her robe until she spotted it on the floor by the front end of the massage table.

"Uh, is everything okay?" Carter asked Mona as she hopped off the table and quickly covered herself.

"Mona, did you hear me, what's wrong?" Carter sat up.

"Yeah, I heard you. Nothing's wrong. I gotta go."

"Okay, but can we—"

Before Carter could say another word, Mona hurried out the door. Carter jumped up, dressed quickly and ran out of the room behind her. He wasn't even a foot from her office door before she slammed it in his face and locked it behind her.

"Mona, open this door and tell me what's wrong. Open the door, please."

"Carter. Please just leave."

"No, not until you tell me what's going on."

"Nothing. I just want to be alone right now."

"Mona, I'd really hate to break this door down, but I will. I swear to God I will."

"Carter, please leave. Just get the hell out of here."

"What is your damn problem? How the hell did we go from having some of the best sex that I've ever had in my life to—to *this*?"

No response.

He pleaded with her for 15 more minutes. He couldn't believe it, but he had been completely shut out. He stared at the door in disbelief.

"Goodnight, Carter." It was like she read his mind.

"Fine. Fuck it, I'm gone." Carter slammed his fists hard against her office door, grabbed the rest of his belongings out of the room, walked out the parlor, fighting the urge to look back.

Mona waited another 10 minutes before she decided to test the waters and make sure the coast was clear. Opening her office door, she stuck her head out to listen, then looked both ways before heading down the hall. She walked calmly back into the red room, pulled the bench from the wall, opened the back of it and grabbed the recorder. Then she stood on the stool, placed it in front of the chest and reached on top of it to grab a second recorder. Placing both of them into her robe pocket, she looked once more before she shut the door behind her. When she stepped back into the hall, she could feel a cool breeze, and as she made her way into the lobby, she saw that Carter had left the door wide open.

"Damn jerk," Mona cursed him.

She pulled it closed and locked it behind her. As she went by the Red Room, she remembered to set the alarm on her phone for two hours from now so she could get up and clean the room before going home for the night. But, for now, she just wanted to wash Carter off of her body and out of her mind.

She needed to brush away any second thoughts about ruining Carter's life because of her emotions—she couldn't afford to be stupid and fall in love with him. She quickly undressed and stepped into the private executive bathroom with the gorgeous stone designed shower.

Turning on her shower radio, Mona heaved a frustrated sigh. She was so deep in thought, using her music to help drown her thoughts that she never heard the supply door closet open from the inside, nor did she hear the back door slam shut.

.

Chapter Eleven

Outside the parlor, Carter jumped into his truck and pulled out his phone. He went to dial Mona's number when his phone rang, never bothering to take a closer look at screen he answered on the first ring.

"Carter."

"Valentine, glad I caught you. I—"

"Hollister, now is not a good time. I'll get back with you first thing in the morning."

"Actually, you don't have to get back to me at all. I will no longer be needing your services."

"Hollister, I'm closing the deal tomorrow at noon," he lied.

"Oh, really?" Hollister asked with a hint of skepticism.

"Yes I am." Carter had never been so annoyed in his life then at the present moment.

"Well still, it's been interesting working with you, but I've decided to handle this takeover personally. So, this concludes our business agreement. You will receive a check of compensation by the end of—"

"Hollister, I saw you earlier with Mona."

"And?"

"And I'm strongly suggesting that you find another business to force out and let Mona be. She's strictly legit."

Hollister chuckled, "Valentine, if you would like to continue to keep your stellar reputation and not be filing for bankruptcy by morning, I strongly suggest that you stay away from business affairs that don't involve you. Especially mine." With that, Hollister ended the call and walked over to his floor to ceiling window that boasted a breathtaking view of downtown Detroit through his spacious condo and contemplated his next move.

Clearly, I've underestimated this Valentine character. A partnership with him would have been ideal. It's too bad that I'm going to have to teach him a lesson in minding his own fuckin business. It's just too damn bad!

****

Turning over on her lounger, Mona glanced at the clock on her desk, then closed her eyes again and snuggled deeper under her throw.

Oh no, please no...

Mona turned back over, sat up and read the clock again.

"Shit! We open in two hours."

Hopping up, she ran out of her office down to the Red Room. Quickly, she cleaned, sanitized, and disinfected the room, almost breaking a sweat to get it back to working order. Noticing most of the oils were too low for her standards, Mona went to replace them. She went to open the supply closet, when she noticed that it had been left slightly ajar. Looking around, Mona suddenly felt uneasy. Pulling the door open toward her, Mona turned on the light and walked inside. Other than the dirty rag bin bag not properly tied around the bin, nothing else looked out of place.

"This is so stupid, I'm paranoid for nothing."

Mona reasoned with herself as she fixed the rag bin, grabbed the oils she came for, and went back to work. As soon as all the rooms were up to par, Mona dressed in a royal blue maxi dress and gold studded flats. Throwing on her smock, she quickly vacuumed and straightened the lobby when her morning staff began making their way into work.

Before she forgot, Mona made a quick detour back to her office. She grabbed the tape she'd copied from Carter's recorder and copies of the ones from last night, as well as a story she'd typed up and placed everything along with a hand written note into a manila envelope and sealed it. Looking down at the envelope, Mona wondered if she was doing the right thing. Last night, while in the shower, she decided to just let karma take care of Carter, but right before her head hit the pillow, she concluded that she was stepping in for Karma, because she personally wanted to make sure Carter paid for trying to take away a dream that she's worked so hard to see come to life.

Yet, here she was again having doubts. A few minutes went by before she had finally come to peace with what she had to do.

"Good morning, ladies."

"Morning, Mona!" the five women greeted simultaneously while making their way back to their work stations to prepare themselves for the day ahead. As soon as Mona flipped the sign on the door from closed to open, patrons entered and began to fill up the lobby immediately.

Though the day ran smoothly, Mona was exhausted and couldn't wait to get home. She just had one more hour before her night manager arrived, and then she would be home free. While checking her appointment log for tomorrow morning, Don's delivery truck pulled into the drive and came in lugging what looked to be a heavy packaging box.

"Good afternoon."

"Afternoon ma'am, I have a special delivery for a Mona Cartwright," the delivery guy read from his tablet.

"I'm Mona Cartwright."

"Alright, can you please sign here?" he asked, pointing to the bottom of the screen as he handed over the mini tablet.

"Here you go, thank you."

"You're welcome. Where would you like for me to place this package?"

"Oh, here next to the stand is fine."

"And your flowers?"

"Flowers, what flowers?"

"I have eight vases of two dozen roses each for you also."

"O-okay, uh…along the shelf by the entrance is fine."

"Alright, be right back."

"Uh, who are the roses from?"

"The customer has instructed that you read the card inside of the box to find out."

"Okay, thanks again."

"No problem."

Mona watched in awe as the delivery guy brought in some of the most breathtakingly beautiful roses that she'd seen since she was a child playing in her grandmother's rose garden.

"Good day, ma'am."

"Same to you."

"Well, what do we have here?" Denise inquired with a smirk as she walked into the parlor and found Mona smelling the roses and smiling.

"It's nothing, so you can get that stupid grin off your face."

"Oh no, I can't honey, not until you tell me how to make a man shower me with my very own rose garden."

"Whatever," Mona laughed as she picked up the box addressed to her that was much lighter than it appeared.

"I'll be in my office for about an hour if you need me."

"Yes boss, but you're going to have to come clean sooner or later."

"Well, it'll definitely be later then."

In her office, Mona set down at her desk and opened the box.

"Oh my, these are so beautiful," she said as she pulled two matching red and black lamps with an image of couples intertwined lovingly, circling the base from the bubble wrap. Carefully, she placed them on her desk, then tore open the card in the red envelope with her name on it.

Hello, pretty lady, I don't know what it is about you, if it's you're smile, the way you seduce a room with your presence, your beauty, or just your personality, but you've got me hook, line, and sinker. I would love to get to know you better, if you're interested, of course. Please enjoy the roses as a token of my appreciation for taking time out of your busy schedule to spend with me. And the lamps because word around town is that they would fit in perfectly with your parlors décor and your sensual personality. Call me when you can, and maybe we can set up a real date this time.

Gram
555-443-4512

Grinning, Mona placed the card on her desk, stood, and began to pace back and forth in the middle of her office.

How sweet! So, he wants a date, huh? I guess I could go... to thank him. That would be the right thing to do, right? But then again, I didn't ask Hollister to buy me these beautiful roses and amazing lamps. Oh, who am I fooling, he seems like a nice guy—but he is no Carter Valentine. Carter...that sexy prick just does something to my soul, not to mention the things he does to the rest of me.

"Good Lord! Mona said as she began to fan herself with her hand.

"No. Yes. No. I mean, no, I will not think about that bastard who is trying to blackmail me and yes, I will go out with Hollister. Even if it's only to take my mind off of Carter. Yeah, that's what I'll do. Just as soon as I come back from Key West on Monday."

*****

Shaun pulled his Explorer in front of Mona's house and jumped out. He knew that she would probably slam the door in his face, but he couldn't let another day go by without explaining everything to her in person. He'd hoped to hear from her after he'd sent the flowers, but deep down, he knew that Mona wanted nothing else to do with him. He hated himself for waiting so long to finally try and make things right, but he still had to try. *Better late than never, right?* With sweaty palms, he rang the doorbell and waited. The main door opened, then after a few moments, the screen door opened slowly and Mona walked out onto the porch. She looked up into Shaun's eyes, then glanced up into the night sky.

"Hello, Mona Lisa," Shaun called her by the nick name he'd given her, explaining to her while they were together that she should've been the original Mona Lisa painting by Leonardo de Vinci.

"Hi," she said as a sudden chill ran up her arms and down her spine.

Walking the length of the porch, she stopped in front of the window and took a seat in the porch swing. Trying to gauge her reaction, Shaun continued to stand in the same spot in front of her door, until she exhaled a deep breath and sat back in the swing. Only then did he tread cautiously and join her.

God, he still smells good, and looks good too.

"Mona Lisa, I'm sorry for just showing up like this, but you left me no choice."

"I left you no choice?" she practically whispered. She closed her eyes and held herself tight before the fat tear drops circling her eyes fell.

"I mean, you never called, and I had to see you to explain to you why I was forced into breaking up with you."

"Shaun, it's a little too late to—"

"Mona Lisa, two minutes, please?"

"One minute. Go."

Shaun ran down what happened, then waited for Mona to respond. After what seemed like forever, she finally responded.

"I am so very sorry for your loss, Shaun, and I'm sorry that your father caused you to lose a good thing. Now that you're wiser, please keep someone else from making the same mistake you did." Mona stood and walked back toward her door.

"Mona Lisa—"

"Shaun, don't—"

"Can I have a hug goodbye?"

Still hugging herself, it took Mona all the strength she could muster to turn around and hug this man that she still loved but was no longer in love with. Stepping into his embrace, he wrapped his arms around her and she hesitantly followed his lead.

"I still love you, Mona Lisa, and I always will."

"And I love you, but I am only interested in moving forward in my life right now." Mona stood on her tippy toes and gently kissed Shaun on the lips. "Good night, Shaun, and goodbye."

Chapter Twelve

"Trina no, please don't cancel on me. I have been waiting on this trip all year," Mona whined into her cell. She had just exited the lodge freeway when her cousin called to give her the bad news.

"I am so sorry, Mona, but I just got the call today about the interview with Cherished Moments photography studios. It's a two-day interview honey, and you know how long I've wanted this call back from them."

"I know, but it still sucks ass, Trina. I don't want to go all by myself! This was our annual girlfriend's trip. I may as well not even go." She pouted as she pulled in front of the Caribbean Chill and Grill restaurant.

"Oh, cut it out, Mona, and take your ass on that damn trip. You just told me the other day that you were starting to feel overwhelmed with everything going on at work and in your personal life. Go, have some fun for a change, do something crazy, live in the moment, then go back to work and act like nothing ever happened."

"Fine, but I just want you to know, I can't stand you."

"Awww, I love you too."

"Whatever, tramp. Well, keep me posted on the interview process, I really hope you get the job. I know how far you've come and how hard you've worked for this."

"Thank you so much, honey. Now, enough with the mushy stuff, go pack 'cause I know you haven't even pulled your suitcase out of your closet yet and turn your ass up in Key West, literally. And when you get back, I want to hear all about it over caramel cheesecake and root beer floats."

"Well, okay, since you're bribing me and everything." Mona pouted.

"Whatever, heifa', I have to go. Love you, and don't forget to call me with all your flight information."

"I will. Love you too. And Trina?"

"Yeah?"

"Good luck, honeybun. But I know you don't need it because God got you."

"Awww! Thanks MoMo, girl."

"Bye." Mona ended the call and sighed.

"Well, I guess it's just me, myself, and I."

Unbuckling her seatbelt, Mona reached into her back seat, grabbed the package that she'd addressed to Carter, and hurried into the post office before she started having second thoughts and changed her mind again. While Mona waited in line to send her package, she scrolled her call log until she found Gram's number and pressed the call button.

"Yes hello, Hollister Gram, please?"

"Well, hello beautiful."

"Hello yourself, handsome."

Hollister didn't give her butterflies like Carter did, but he still made her smile.

"I take it you received the roses and the lamps and that you want me to whisk you away to Barbados with me?"

"Yes, I did receive the beautiful gifts, thank you very much. They had me grinning that entire afternoon. But as relaxing as that sounds, I'm going to have to pass on Barbados. At least for now, anyway."

"Well, that's alright. I'm just happy I could bring that beautiful smile out to play. And the whole Barbados thing was worth a try, but at least you didn't say no!" Hollister laughed.

"No woman in her right mind would turn down a trip to the islands with a handsome man."

"Mona, I'm so happy that you can't see me over here blushing like a school girl. Woman, you're dangerous."

"Just a little bit."

"So, Barbados may be too soon, but how about dinner tomorrow night at Andiamo's on the Riverfront?"

"That sounds amazing, but I'm heading out of town later on tonight and won't be returning until Monday morning. But if the offer still stands when I get back, I would love to join you for dinner that night."

"Oh, it definitely still stands. I'll see you Monday night."

She nodded. "Until Monday."

****

"Another Remy on the rocks when you get a minute." Carter signaled the bartender behind the bar at Floods.

"Coming right up."

What in the hell is wrong with me?

Carter had been at Floods for the last two hours trying to figure out when he had allowed himself to care so much for a woman, let alone worry about what the hell was bothering her. Carter had called Mona several times since she locked herself in her office but still no word from her in the last few days. He had no idea why or what he'd done wrong. He had only known the woman for a month, and she was driving him crazy.

"Women," he mumbled as the bartender placed his third drink in front of him.

"Thanks." Grabbing the glass, he took a few sips while he surveyed the bar. It was a nice crowd, not too packed, but just right for him to get a good buzz going, hear some of the best jazz in Detroit, and meet a sexy lady. Though tonight, with the exception of oblivious hookers and the women that weren't his type, every other woman was taken.

"Damn, where are all the women? Preferably those who are the total opposite of Mona." Slipping his hand into his suit pants pocket, Carter pulled out his phone and dialed Mona's number again. And again, there was no answer.

"Well, at least she's not sending me to voicemail like she was doing earlier," he mumbled to himself.

Shaking his head, Carter downed the rest of his drink and tried his best to enjoy the atmosphere, but after another hour of feeling like shit, he decided to head home and call it a night.

"Tomorrow, Mona is going to explain herself, or I'll seduce a confession out of her. Yeah, that's what I'll do," he laughed at his own lame joke as he pulled in his driveway.

Heading up his walkway, he was so out of it that he almost didn't see the package setting on his doorstep. Inspecting the package that had no return address on it, he carried it inside and tossed it on his coffee table in front of his couch.

"Whatever it is can wait until morning," he said as he stripped naked, swiped the half empty bottle of tequila from the kitchen island, and headed upstairs to the shower.

****

"You guess you were *wrong*? That's all you got to say?" Shaun asked as he sat across from his father at Tom's Oyster Bar on Jefferson.

"Son, what else do you want me to say? I gave you my opinion of the situation at the time, and that was that settling down was not the thing for you. Turns out, I was wrong to give you that advice, but I can't turn back time. On the flip side, you are wealthy and a well-respected Chemical Engineer. So, the way I see it, I *did* do something right." He took a swig of his Miller Light.

"Ha, I wish I knew that you were jealous of me—of your own damn son. You're pathetic."

"Excuse me, Shaun, you better lighten up on that Patron you're throwing back before—"

No, I know exactly what I'm saying. Stop blaming other people for your mistakes. I've always respected and looked up to you until this moment. I just realized what a big coward you really are."

"Alright, that's enough." His father slammed his hand down on the table.

"No, it's not. Stop blaming everyone else because mom left you because you weren't ready to settle down with one woman or get married! How are you going to keep your own son from—man, I'm out of here." Shaun stood and dropped a few bills on the table to cover their drinks and the tip, then he made his way to the exit.

"Shaun?"

"What, pop?"

"I'm sorry."

"Yeah, you sure are."

****

"Thank God that's over," Mona mumbled as she had just left the security checkpoint area feeling somewhat violated. Putting the ordeal behind her, she stopped in a small convenient store, purchased a Fuji water then proceeded to wheel her red suitcase down to gate number 20.

"Hello." Mona smiled and handed over her ticket to the boarding ticket booth attendant.

"Hello. Have a safe flight and enjoy your trip."

"Thanks." Once she settled into her window seat and looked around, she was relieved that this wasn't a packed flight and that the seat next to her was vacant. As soon as the flight attendant and pilot made the necessary announcements, they were off, non-stop to Florida, and no sooner had Mona placed her headphones in her ears and stretched her legs across the empty seat, she fell fast asleep.

A little over an hour later, Mona jerked awake from a deep sleep and nervously glanced around. As her surroundings slowly began to come into focus and she remembered where she was, her heart rate slowly returned to normal. Placing her hand over her chest, Mona tried remembering the dream that had just jolted her awake. She couldn't remember exactly what happened in the dream, but she did remember Shaun and Hollister watching Carter make love to her on a beach. Startled, but turned on by the vivid imagery, Mona pulled her tablet from her tote and began to surf the net. After about five minutes, of trying to stay focused, she powered down her iPad and tried to go back to sleep.

Only this time, as soon as she closed her eyes, she saw her and Carter on the beach again, but this time, there was no audience. The way he was taking her over and over and the way her body responded to him was enough to drive her insane with need. Squeezing her thighs together, Mona tried to stop her clit from throbbing. But the harder she squeezed, the worse the throbbing became.

"Damn him! But I want him soooo bad!"

Skimming the plane, Mona took note that the back half of the plane was asleep, while the front half was either reading or otherwise occupied. Content with what she saw, she pulled a big red sack from her tote and rumbled around inside until she found her favorite remote control vibrator that she'd ordered from Pure Romance, better known as the Hanky Panky. Kissing the vibrator, Mona spread her thighs, pulled her leggings away from her body, and tried not to moan too loudly as she slipped her vibrator inside of her. She grinned at how soaked she was, she couldn't wait to cum hard and fast. Reaching for the remote to Mr. Hanky Panky, she did a once over of the plane once more to make sure no one could see what she was doing or walking down the aisle.

Excited, she pressed the power button and nothing happened. Thinking she hit the speed button instead of the power button, she held up the remote and made sure to press the power button, still nothing happened. Annoyed, Mona cursed and prayed at the same time while flipping over the remote to check and rotate the batteries. Snapping the back shell back in place, she turned the toy on again and finally the vibrator begin to buzz inside of her. And just as quickly, it powered down again.

"No, this cannot be happening to me right now. Shit! Why didn't I think to pack some damn batteries? Fuck."

Pissed that she couldn't cum, she leaned over to pull the vibrator from her wet pussy when she spotted a professional Nikon camera sticking out of the Nike bag next to the man in the seat in front of her. Mona started to tap the man on the shoulders and kindly ask him if he would sell her the batteries, but when she realized he was deep asleep, she decided to "borrow" them. She waited until the stewardess did her walk thru then slowly slid her hand around the seat and into his bag that the man's arm was wrapped securely around. As luck would have it, when she reached into the bag, her hand landed on an unopened pack of batteries. Wrapping her fingers around the package, she slowly pulled and was almost home free when the man stirred slightly and tightened his grasp on his bag. Her heart went into overdrive as panic immediately overtook her. She breathed a sigh of relief when the owner turned his head toward the window, but never woke up.

Quickly, Mona pushed the camera away from the batteries and pulled them from the bag.

"Whew!" She mouthed.

Ripping over the pack of Energizer batteries, she popped four in and switched on the remote again. The Hanky Panky vibrantly came to life as it instantly began rotating and jumping in her drenched pussy.

"Ohhh, yes," Mona moaned just as a passenger walked by. The second they made eye contact, Mona knew that what she thought was a soft whisper of a moan was really louder than she intended. Making a mental note to keep it down, she jacked the speed and bit her bottom lip when the vibrator began massaging her clit, walls, and g-spot all at the same time.

"Fuck me. Yesss. Oh Carter, you feel so good. Fuckkkk," she panted as she shivered uncontrollably and came hard all over herself, just as the plane landed on the runway.

****

Hollister sat in his car with his phone to his ear, smoking a blunt outside his auntie's house waiting for his longtime friend and college roommate to answer the other end. He dreaded making this phone call all day, but he had to let Shaun know that their deal was off because not only did he like Mona, he was falling for her hard. Hollister believed that there was more to what Shaun told him about Mona stealing from him a few years back, but Shaun was his boy, so he asked no questions. This was his brother from another mother, and they had each other's backs for years. This would be the first time in their friendship that there was ever a rift between them.

"Hello?"

"Shaun, what's good?"

"I'm hanging, dude. What's the word?"

"Listen man, I got to back out of that little arrangement we had to takeover that parlor."

"Why man, what's up, what happened? You letting that bitch get the best of you?"

"Naw man, I just can't do it. It don't feel right."

"Dude, what you mean? I paid you a lot of money to handle this. I paid you a lot of money to snatch that fucking parlor out from under her shady ass."

"Whoa, Shaun, you really need to chill. And you can have the money back. I thought I'd give you a courtesy call, but I see this was a mistake."

"Courtesy? Gram, fuck courtesy! Do what the fuck I paid you to do or your punk ass is going back to lock up."

"Shaun, you don't want to make threats that you can't follow through on. And don't forget I went to lock up to cover for yo' ass. So, you really need to tone all that big talk down."

"Who said I can't follow through? And fuck what you did for me back then, what have you done for me lately? Not a mutherfucking thing, bro. You got 72 hours, or you going to be doing 25 to life."

"Shaun man, I don't know what the fuck is up with you, but if you start fucking with my freedom, my life, I swear your throat will be slit by morning. The damn deal is off, get the fuck over it, and move on or do your fucking dirty work on your own."

****

Carter sat up in his bed and slammed his eyes shut. His head was pounding. He hadn't had a headache this painful in years. Rising from the bed, he looked down to slide his feet into his house shoes, but they weren't in his usual spot by his bed. As he searched his room, he wondered why he only wore a towel wrapped around his waist, his phone was in the tub, and an empty bottle of tequila was laying on the floor in his closet.

In too much pain to care at the moment, he took the steps to his staircase two at a time until he made it to his kitchen. Grabbing the brand new bottle of Ibuprofen from the counter, he downed two of the painkillers dry before treading carefully into his living room and flopping down in his black lazy boy recliner. After 20 minutes of just staring out of his front window and trying to figure out where in the hell the tan package that was sitting in the center of his living room table come from, his memories finally started coming back to him.

Sitting up in his seat, he leaned forward and pulled the package toward him. Wondering who sent it, he flipped the package over to see who it was from and saw a blank space where a return address should have been. "Who in the hell is this from?"

A few more moments passed of beating himself up with wonder before he finally just ripped through the heavy-duty envelope and bubble wrap and pulled everything out. Looking strangely at the tape again, he wondered who it was from and what was on it, until he unfolded and read the letter attached to it.

Greetings Valentine,

I guess you really meant what you said about doing everything you can to acquire my property. To go as far as to blackmail me by having sex with you was low. Even for a piece of no good scum such as yourself. But you see, two can play that game, Valentine, especially when you leave evidence behind. I was pissed when I found the tape at first, but when I calmed down and came more times than I can remember, I became clearheaded enough to come up with a plan of blackmail of my own.

I thought I'd send you one of the many copies of the tape that I've made to you just to show you that I'm not bluffing and so you can look real closely at the copy before it's altered along with the other tape that I recorded the last night we were in the Red Room. I think I'll be sending that one directly to every local media outlet that will listen to my story of how the big time real estate mogul is impotent and can only get off by blackmailing women into having sex with them in his storage closet—in his basement.

I believe this is a checkmate, Mr. Valentine. You have a wonderful day.

Mona

P.S. You should probably watch your back from here on out.

"Shit! No. no. no. Mona. Fuck, I gotta stop her!"

Crumpling up the letter, Carter jumped up, ran to his room, and slipped into a pair of jeans and a white tee. He grabbed his keys and running shoes from his front closet and hurried out the door. Jumping in the car, he threw his shoes across the seat and sped all the way across town. He called Mona repeatedly on her cell on the way over but it was to no anvil.

I've never ran so many lights in my entire life, he thought as he flew into the Soothing Touch parking lot. He was moving so fast, he nearly missed the side of the building because he forgot to put his car into park. Quickly, he jammed his foot on the break and slid himself back into the driver's seat, yanked the break in park, and stormed through the entrance.

"Excuse me. Excuse me, sir!" Carter yelled as he made his way to the front of the long line of patrons waiting to be serviced.

"Excuse me, Mr. Valentine, what are you doing?" Jayme, the morning receptionist pulled him aside and asked through gritted teeth. You know you have to wait in line like everyone else."

"I don't want no damn massage, Jayme. I need to speak to Mona now. So, go get her and tell her to get her ass out here right now."

"I'm sorry, but she isn't here." Jayme softened her tone hoping to calm Carter and keep him from making an even bigger scene.

"Fine, I'll wait."

"Mr. Valentine, she isn't coming back anytime soon. She's out of town on vacation until Tuesday. If you like, I could give her a call as soon as I clear my line."

"Don't bother."

Carter was so angry, he slammed the glass door open so hard when he stormed out, it cracked and shattered against the concrete wall behind it.

****

A little after one in the morning, Carter pulled up to Mona's house. Once he thought he'd gathered his thoughts, he decided to pull all the way up into the driveway as not to be clearly identified should someone see what he was about to do. Reading the address that his friend hacked for him earlier that afternoon, he scrolled down the screen and quickly looked at the alarm code once more then exited his car. Glancing over his shoulder, he checked to make sure the coast was clear before he walked up to Mona's back door. Kneeling down, Carter pulled a handful of tools from his pocket. Then, he sat them down on the grass next to a row of potted plants and raised up to open the screen door.

"Shit. Who locks their screen door?" he mumbled as he grabbed a flat head screwdriver and his Swiss army knife from the ground.

After a few maneuvers, the screen door clicked open giving way to the main door. Seeing he had a much more difficult task on his hand with the second door, Carter reached for a pick from his tension pick set. When he went to pick up one of the picks, the rod caught a piece of what he thought was a branch at first, but upon closer inspection, he realized it was a small metal pole sticking out of the ground directly behind the potted plant closest to the door. Carter sat down to further inspect the pole with his flashlight when he finally ran out of patience and pulled it from the ground. When it was ejected, a rubber band with a key was attached to the other end. Looking at what he'd uncovered, Carter smiled and said, "It can't be."

Snapping the key from the band, he stood up and stuck the key in the lock and turned the lock and smiled again as he turned the knob and opened the door. Immediately, the alarm went off as it told him that the police were on their way. Making his way to the key pad, he quickly punched in the number that he'd memorized that his friend had given him, and the blaring warning call instantly came to an end. Turning on the light over the sink, Carter took in his surroundings before shutting the side door and finally getting down to business. Starting in the kitchen, Carter went from room to room, checking all three bedrooms and both baths of Mona's ranch style home. He was looking for any indication of where Mona might have gone for vacation.

30 minutes later, Carter hadn't found so much as a receipt with her plane ticket or airline information anywhere in her home. Frustrated, Carter sat down on the side of Mona's bed when he noticed the smell of mint and roses throughout her room. The smell of her room and her deep red walls that were only this color in her room, reminded him of how seductive and sensual his woman was without even trying to be.

Damn, did I really just say my woman? Why can't I get this woman out of my head? Carter shook his head and stood.

He walked to her dresser and finished searching for something with the information he desperately needed. When he turned up nothing on her dresser, he pulled the top left drawer opened and he wished he hadn't. He'd never seen so much lingerie and so many dildos and vibrators in his life. And apparently, this Pure Romance Company was her all-time favorite as the logo was on 80 percent of the toys in the drawer. Quickly, Carter closed the drawer and moved across the hall into Mona's home office, and the last room in the house he needed to check before he gave up on this search.

Taking his time, Carter went through every desk drawer, file cabinet, bookcase, and cubby hole in her small office and still came up empty. Flipping through some papers on her desk in a stack of trays, he dropped a paperweight on her keyboard and her computer popped on. And there on her screen was Mona's travel itinerary, complete with hotel and car rental information.

"Bingo."

Replacing the paperweight in the stand, he grabbed a sticky note, jotted down the itinerary, and made his way out of the back out the side door. As he was leaving, he pulled out his Galaxy Note 2 and placed a call to Metro Airport.

"Hello, I need to catch a red eye tonight to Key West."

Chapter Thirteen

Shaun sat on the bench at Belle Isle Park tossing the remaining pieces of his chicken shawarma to the birds. Every few moments, he would look over his shoulder to see if a red Impala pulled up and parked at the curb behind his Mustang. While taking in the amazing view of the Detroit River, he heard a car pull up and the engine die a few moments after. As the petite figure with the blond braids approached, Shaun inwardly breathed a sigh of relief.

"Well, hello handsome. Don't you look all kinds of sexy today," the woman said as she licked and bit her bottom lip.

"Dee Dee, where have you been? You were supposed to be 30 minutes ago."

"Honey bump, my nail appointment ran a little late, and I had to stop at the post office," she said as she took a seat on the bench next to him.

"Whatever, do you have anything that I can use to shut the parlor down?"

"Not exactly."

"What do you mean, not exactly? Its either 'yes I do' or 'no I don't'."

"Well, if your grumpy ass would let me explain, you'd understand."

"Okay, you're right. I'm sorry, I'm just having a bad day, baby. Come here." Dee Dee scooted closer to him until they were elbow to arm and Shaun gently placed a soft kiss to her lips.

"Now, tell me what's going on?" he urged as he ran his hand across her thigh.

Content with his apology, she began, "Okay, so I searched Mona's office and found nothing that could be used to shut her down. But, while looking, I got locked in the parlor and heard her fucking this real estate guy that's been snooping around lately. I had to hide in the supply closet and stay there until they finished. I was so fucking horny listening to them. He was giving it to her good, too..."

"Dee Dee. Point? And how in the hell is her fucking anybody helping me?" He acted annoyed. But inwardly, he was pissed the fuck off.

"Okay, the point is, she recorded it, because when I snuck to the door to try to take pictures, I saw a recorder light turn on. I tried to grab it, but when her head started to turn toward the door, I took off. Then when they were done and I went back, the recorder was gone. And I couldn't go search in her office because she had locked herself in there. He really must've fucked up though because I think he's the one who sent her a bunch of flowers the next day. Baby, why don't you send me flowers?"

"Dee Dee, we can talk about that later, can you get the tape of her and the dude fucking?"

"I can try, honey. But you know it's going to cost you, right?" She smiled right before she went in for a kiss, tongue first.

"Whatever you want, baby, it's yours. Just please try and get me that tape. How soon do you think it'll be?"

"Well, I go back to work tomorrow. I'll try then."

"Okay, great. Baby, you are the best."

"Shaun, if I can get this tape, can I finally quit? You told me that I only had to get the receptionist position and befriend Mona and then I could quit and we could finally be together."

"Baby, if you can get me that video, we can be together and you can quit."

"You mean it, Shaun?"

"I mean it, baby."

"Good baby, because I can't stand that uppity bitch."

****

"Oh yeah, now this is paradise," Mona exhaled as she opened the door and walked into her spacious, all white suite at the beautiful Ocean Key Resort in Key West. Dropping her luggage, Mona kicked the door closed and ran from room to room like a kid in a new home smiling, from ear to ear.

"All mine! All weekend!" she screamed as she ran in the master bedroom and fell back across the bed. After a few moments, she sat up and glanced around the room the walked back into the common area and stood.

"But I'm all alone. Damn you, Trina," she mumbled.

She grabbed the remote to her 52-inch TV and fell back onto the white modern sectional. She clicked on the television and put her feet up on the coffee table. "Oh well, I may be all alone, but I'm sure I can find all kinds of fun to get into, and I always have Mr. Hanky Panky to keep me entertained." She smiled as she jumped up and headed for the shower.

One long, very relaxing shower later, Mona dressed in an all red one-piece swimsuit with the sides cut out, except for the double lines of gold wrapped around it. She slid her matching sarong and flip flops on and headed out the door. Mona got all the way to the elevator before she realized that she'd left her sunglass and favorite lip gloss.

"Damn." She headed quickly back to her hotel room. Once there, she quickly grabbed her items and made her way back to the door. While pulling the door open, she dropped her shades and when she stood upright and walked out the door, she came face to face with Carter. Startled, she jumped back and grabbed her chest.

"Holy shit! You scared the fuck out of me. What the hell are you doing here, Carter?"

"Mona, we need to talk."

"No, we don't. Now, if you'll excuse me." She tried to push past Carter, but he never moved an inch.

"Carter, I really don't have time for this right now. In case you haven't noticed, I'm on a mini-vacation, damn it!"

"Mona, we really—"

"I don't want to talk to your shady ass! Now get the hell out of my way before I call security. Wait." She took a step back and pointed her finger in his face. "How in the hell did you know I was here? I—Oh my God, you're stalking me!"

Mona took off toward her suite phone, but before she could call anyone, Carter was behind her and snatched the phone from her, ripped the cord from the wall, and tossed it on the couch. Thinking quickly, Mona ran for her phone on the table in the lobby when Carter picked her up and carried her over to the couch.

"Put me the fuck down you fucking crazy ass psycho! Help! Somebody help me!!!" she screamed.

Sitting down, he pulled Mona into his lap and held her there. Her struggle to break free only excited him. "If you keep up all that screaming, Mona, I'm going to give you one hell of a reason to scream."

Instantly, Mona's mouth snapped shut.

"Thank you. Now, what did you do with the tape?"

"Like I'm going to tell you, especially after you tried to blackmail me with it! I'm not telling you shit." Carter kissed Mona on the back of her neck, then traveled down her bare back.

"Carter, what are you doing?"

"Kissing you."

"Why?"

"Because I want to. You smell so damn good."

"Carter?"

"Yes?" he asked as he trailed his tongue back up Mona's back. Then he gently caressed her arms.

"I don't want you kissing me." She shivered.

"Yes you do."

"No. I don't."

"Then why are you moaning?"

"I -ohhhh." *What the hell? I'm moaning. How long have I been doing this?*

"What was that?" Carter asked as he slipped the left strap of her swimsuit over her shoulder and began to kiss her there. He then did the same thing to her right side.

"I—don't..."

Carter didn't wait for her to finish her sentence. He pulled her back and slipped a nipple into his mouth.

"Caaaarterrr...." she purred.

"I'm here, baby," he said, her nipple still in his mouth.

"Carter, no. I—I don't want this."

"Fine," Carter huffed. He was pissed and he was going to make sure she knew just how much.

"Mona," Carter started after a few moments of them both wrestling each other around on the couch. "It's not what you think. I—"

"So, you're telling me that you *didn't* mean to blackmail me?"

"No. Yes. I mean, I was going to blackmail you at first, but I decided not to. I wanted the movie to keep for myself," he whispered, slightly embarrassed.

"Well, I don't believe you. And would you please let me go, I'm not comfortable sitting on your lap." Even though he preferred Mona to stay exactly where she was, he moved her into the spot next to him.

"If you run, I'll make sure you regret it," Carter said as he let her go.

For some reason, Mona believed his every word and as a result, didn't move a single inch. She'd come to learn that Carter meant every word he said. Filtering out the dirty images of Carter taking her over and over again, she finally found a corner of her mind that hadn't been corrupted and refocused on the topic at hand.

"You wanted to put me out of business so bad that you would blackmail me? Do you know how hard I've worked to open and run a legitimate and profitable business? I've worked hard to make my dream what it is today and you're trying to take it from me. Why? And I know you're working with somebody as corrupt as you are."

She crossed her arms.

"Mona, I'm sorry. I was going to blackmail you, but had a change of heart. I was coming to tell you everything yesterday, but you were gone."

"What made you change your mind?"

"You."

"What? What do you mean, 'me'?"

"You. I'm falling for you hard, and the last thing I want to do is hurt you. I want to get to know you better. Surprisingly, you've become very important to me in this short amount of time. I thought I wanted your business…but not anymore."

Mona was speechless. This was the last thing she expected to ever hear from Carter. "How do I know this is not some ploy to get me to tell you what I did with the videos?"

"It's not, I—. You said *videos*, I only recorded one. Awww, shit, Mona, what have you done?" Carter asked.

"No, what have *you* done? This is all *your* fault."

"You're right, I'm sorry, but you need to tell me what you did with the tapes because if Hollister gets his hands on those, we could both lose everything."
"What did you just say?"

"I'm serious. We could lose—"

"No, about Hollister? What does he have to do with all this?"

"He's the one who hired me to take over your business and turn it into a parlor."

"What?"

"You didn't know?"

"No, I didn't. How in the hell would I have known that?"

"Well, when I saw you two at the Elise's, I thought you knew. I thought you were the reason he fired me."

"He *fired* you?"

"Yes. And he didn't take too kindly when I told him to back off of you."

"Why would you tell him that?"

"Mona, not right now. We can discuss that later. Where are the videos?"

"I sent them to my cousin's to have them edited, then I instructed her to send them to the media afterwards."

"You did *what*??"

Hollister sat in the waiting area at Gary's car care on Woodward at West Grand Boulevard, trying to control his anger until he was alone. Thing was, he wouldn't be going anywhere for the next couple of hours while his mechanic repaired all the damage going on under the hood. It was just four hours ago, at six this morning that Hollister had come outside and hopped into his corvette on his way to work to find that it wouldn't start. Jumping out, he popped the hood and found that his car had been tampered with.

He thought of Shaun immediately. *Was he really that pissed that he'd backed out of their deal?* Hollister wondered. He refused to believe that as long as they'd been friends, Shaun would do anything to try to harm him. Aside from this issue that they were currently having, he and Shaun had never had so much as even a disagreement. They'd been friends for the last 13 years, and he refused to believe Shaun had anything to do with this. He also believed that there was much more to him and Mona that he wasn't telling him.

Did Mona really steal money from Shaun? Maybe he could get the truth from Mona when she got back in town. But with the way he'd been feeling about Mona, Hollister didn't know if he really wanted to hear the truth.

It didn't take long for Hollister's thoughts to completely focus on Mona and their pre-planned date. Pulling his phone from his pocket, Hollister dialed Mona's number and waited for her to answer. He needed to temporarily take his mind off his troubles and was hoping that the sound of Mona's voice would do the trick.

"Hello?"

"Hello beaut..."

"Carter don't, please," Mona whispered.

"Hello? Mona?"

"Hollister, how are you?"

"I'm well. Are you enjoying your vacation?"

"Very much so. Listen, can I call you back in about an hour, is that okay?"

"Sure, talk to you soon."

"Okay, great." Mona ended the call with the dial tone.

Did she say Carter? As in Carter Valentine? Is this why he told me to stay away from Mona? Hollister wondered as he stared down at his phone.

Well, dude is sadly mistaken if he thinks I'm going to just back off.

"Hollister?"

"Yeah Gary, how bad is the damage?" he asked as he stood.

"You're going to need a new engine, and if I may suggest, you watch your back and call the police. This was done intentionally."

"Are you sure, man?"

"Positive. And if I were you, I would be sending off prayers to the high heavens because had you gotten the car started, you wouldn't be here right now."

"How long before you get the new engine?"

"Three days before it's even delivered and another day for labor."

"Alright, go ahead and take care of everything for me, Gary."

"You got it, Hollister. I'll give you a call when it's ready."

"Thanks, man." Hollister nodded as he headed across the street to the Enterprise rental car company, trying to sort out the disappointing and dangerous turn of events.

****

"Who the fuck is Carter Valentine?" Shaun spat out, as he paced alongside his car in the garage.

He had pulled into to his driveway 30 minutes ago and still had not entered his home because he was so angry about the news that Denise had just shared with him a few hours ago. "That's why we can't get back together because this damn dude is all in her fucking space. Well, it looks like I'm going to have to pay this Carter person a visit and have a man-to-man before he pisses me off. And if that

106

won't work, I'll just have to have to take a look under the hood of his car as well." He banged his fist on his hood and walked inside his home.

As soon as Shaun locked his side door behind him, his phone began ringing. Reading the screen, he shook his head and hit the vibrate button. As soon as the phone stopped vibrating, it started right back up again a minute later. Sending the caller to voicemail this time, the buzzing stopped immediately. But again, began ringing for the third time in less than five minutes. Seething, Shaun snatched up his IPhone and stabbed the talk button. "Denise, I am in the middle of a very important meeting, I'll call you back when went it's over." He quickly ended the call before she could reply.

He was so tired of Denise and couldn't wait until all this shit with Mona was over because Denise was becoming a real pain in his ass. Shaun's plan was to get rid of her a long time ago, but when his original plan to get back Mona failed, he had to keep her around to do his dirty work until Mona came to her senses. Shaun had met Denise one night while leaving the Cigar Bar in Midtown. The second he laid eyes on her in that black bodysuit he wanted to slid up in her.

He wanted sex and nothing more, and he was about to tell her just that after he followed her back to her place and fucked her on the couch in her loft. But when she told him she loved him, he decided that if she loved him that fast, he could get her to do anything for him, including helping him get back the only woman he wanted to be with. He'd lied and told Denise that he wanted to marry her, but that he couldn't because his old business partner, Mona, had stolen a lot of money from him and that he needed her to help him get it back. Then, they could finally be together.

He talked her into applying for the receptionists gig at Mona's parlor to keep an eye on her for him. Everything was going smoothly at first, but she had since become so clingy, wanting to know his every move and why he didn't answer her phone calls quick enough for her. If something didn't give soon, he'd have to cut Denise loose and come up with another plan to help get Mona back. Grabbing a Bud Light from the fridge, Shaun walked into the living room and fell back onto the couch.

"I could've finally gotten rid of that clingy bitch had it not been for Hollister backing out of buying the Soothing Touch." He needed Hollister to purchase the building with the threat to convert it into a cafe, so he could then buy the building for Mona.

"Take away everything she has. Then give her everything she needs," Shaun quoted Eddie Murphy in the movie, *Vampire in Brooklyn*.

"Fucking bastard is going to pay for that shit," he seethed. "He's lucky I didn't have enough time to completely fuck up his ride last night." If the police hadn't been snooping around his neighborhood, he would've made sure Hollister had to get a new ride. He wanted to inconvenience his life since Hollister had inconvenienced him.

"Payback is a bitch, bastard."

****

"Mona, tell me you're kidding?"

"I most certainly am not."

"Why would you do—"

"I know you're not about to fix your lips to ask me why I would go through such great lengths to give you a taste of your own medicine. You threaten my livelihood and I'm in the wrong? You have got some nerve, Carter." Mona stood and walked out onto the balcony.

Moments later, Carter walked up behind her. For a while, no words were exchanged, only the sound of soft breathing as they took in the beautiful Key West night life. About 15 minutes later, Carter broke the silence.

"Mona, even though my original intention was to blackmail you for money, somewhere along the way, just the thought of you changed my plans. I couldn't go through with it. The same night I was going to tell Hollister I couldn't do it, he fired me. I thought you knew when I saw you two that afternoon at the donut shop." He walked up to her and turned her to face him.

"Woman, I am crazy about you. And as crazy as it sounds, I'm happy Hollister hired me or I never would've met you. I want you Mona. All of you all the time. Please believe me when I say that I am so sorry I hurt you."

"Why did Hollister ask you?"

"Not to sound full of myself, but I am very good at my job. Somehow, Hollister found me and told me what he wanted and that money was no object. He did try to get me to buy you out first, though, but when you wouldn't budge, he told me to do whatever I had to do get you out because he needed the property by a certain date."

"Did he say why he wanted my parlor, but not the cafe?"

"No. He was very adamant on your location, though."

"I don't get it. He could've chose any building that wasn't occupied and for next to nothing. Why mine?"

"Honestly, I was so wrapped up in the money that I never gave it any thought until he fired me. Then I started looking at it like a blessing in disguise because something smelled shady when I thought back on everything. So, I'm glad I'm no longer associated with him. But, I feel like it's not over between him and I. Mona, please, you have to get those recordings back."

"Okay. I will, but I swear if you're lying to me, those tapes are going to be the least of your worries."

"Ha, you make a lot of threats for such a little woman."

"I know. I do big business, though." They chuckled.

"I wonder what the hell Hollister wants with me. I told him that I owned the parlor, but he never said anything about wanting to buy my parlor. He never said anything about what he did either. But he did smile almost devilishly when I told him I owned the Soothing Touch. Now that you've told me all of this, something just doesn't feel right."

"I know. I could have a friend look into him for you when we get back home, if you'd like."

"I'd like that very much, *Valentine*. But uh, you said, when 'we' get back. I don't recall coming on this vacation with *you*."

"Yeah, well I thought you could use a friend."

"Did you now?"

"I did."

"How in the hell did you know exactly where to find me anyway?"

"Uh, don't get mad—but I—um…went to break into your house, but I found your spare key in the dirt. I searched your house until I found something on it with your whereabouts. If you hadn't left your email open, I would've had of gone to your office at work and broke in there until I found what I needed."

"You didn't mess up anything in my house, did you?"

"No. Did you lock the door back and turn the alarm back on?"

"Yes."

"Okay."

"That's it, you're not mad?"

"Oh, I wouldn't say all that. Under any other circumstances, I'd be pissed and press charges the first chance I got, but I would have probably done the same thing or something much worse if someone had something in their possession that could end my career. Although, I am very disturbed and a little horrified that you have so many stalker tendencies, but I will admit that somewhere in my twisted, warped mind, I'm actually happy you're here. And that blackmail is all that Hollister had planned for me."

"I know you have no way of knowing this, especially since we haven't known each other long, but I would never intentionally hurt you in any way."

"I feel it." She wrapped her arms around his neck. "For some reason, I feel perfectly safe around you. Trust me, if I didn't, I would've reached for my stun gun or my knives, or my lighter fluid or my—"

"Did you just say lighter fluid?"

"I sure did."

"What in the hell are you going to do with that?"

"What would you do if someone poured it on you?"

"Woman, you are something else."

"You have no idea."

"I'm beginning to see a lot of things I had no idea about when it comes to you. For example, I knew you would probably look great in a swimsuit, but I had no idea that you would far supersede my expectations. You look downright amazing."

"Why thank you," Mona began. She made her way back into the suite and walked into the kitchen, grabbed a bottled water, and gulped it down. She tossed the empty bottle at him as he trailed into the kitchen behind her. "But you should see me naked."

"You're right, take off that swimsuit."

"And why would I do that?" She grinned.

"So I can see you naked like you said."

"I said you *should* see me naked, not that I was going to show you."

"Then why you even suggest it?"

"Well, look at me, it was only the right thing to do."

"No, the right thing to do would be for you to do is spread your legs and try not to scream when I walk over to you, rip that flimsy suit from your body, and have my way with you on the balcony."

"And if I don't, 'do the right thing'?"

Carter walked up to Mona, pulled her until his chest crushed her breasts and said, "I am going to assist you to ensure that you do."

Before Mona could utter another witty remark, Carter ended it with a soft kiss to her lips. Reaching around, he placed a hand on the back of her neck and slipped his tongue between her lips. He didn't want her to think, just feel. Mona instantly welcomed him to come and mate with her tongue. As she grabbed his waist, Carter ground his dick into the softness between her thighs. Coming up for air briefly, Carter started a trail of kisses that began at her chin then traveled the length of her neck and all the way down her breasts.

Mona's moans were music to his ears as she gave him full control of her body. Carefully, Carter backed her up until her soft ass was crushed between him and the counter. He slid both straps of Mona's swimsuit from her shoulders, and he kissed her there before continuing his journey downward as he dropped to his knees.

Stopping momentarily at her beasts, Carter took a black pebbled peak into his mouth and sucked gently, but deeply before catering to her other nipple.

"Ooooh, yes..." She held his head in place.

Carter couldn't take any more of the self-inflicted torture he was currently experiencing as his dick was trying to bust through his pants and jump into Mona's wetness. With his lips still wrapped around her right breast, Carter yanked the rest of her swimsuit off, spread her legs, and ran his fingers between her smoldering heat.

"Oh fuck," Carter whispered as Mona's nipple slipped from his mouth.

Standing up right, Carter unbuckled his pants, letting them fall to the floor. He picked Mona up, pinned her against the kitchen wall, and slipped inside of her wetness.

"Ohhhhh," they both moaned simultaneously as they became one. They found an addictive groove just as Mona bit down on Carter's shoulder and screamed out in between thrusts. This was the beginning of the end for him just as his dick somewhat gotten even harder as he pummeled and pounded and shot them right up through the clouds.

"Oh fuck. Yess." As mixing mumbled calls of passion and expletives mingled with heavy breathing, they found their cloud and came together.

"Mona, you ready for round two?" Carter smiled as his breathing slowly turned to normal.

"Me? Are you ready? You're the one still trying to catch your breath."

Backing away from the wall, Carter made his way toward the

very inviting king sized bed while still inside of Mona. His dick hard all over again.

"I'm going to show you and that smart mouth of yours just how ready I am, all night long."

Laying her down in the center of the bed, Carter slipped out of Mona long enough to replace his manhood with his lips. And he never heard another smart mouth remark from her for the rest of the night, or early the next morning.

Chapter Fifteen

Denise grinned like a fox in a hen house as she practically skipped her way into Soothing Touch half an hour before everyone else was scheduled to arrive. Thanks to Jayme for needing to switch shifts with her at the last minute, she didn't even have to think of a way to get into Mona's office without curious stares or witnesses. After disarming the security system, Denise locked the door behind her and made her way to the receptionist stand. Kneeling down, she pulled the bottom drawer, opened it, pulled out the metal box inside, and spun the combination she needed to get access. Once the lock popped, she grabbed the small white envelope and removed the key to Mona's office in the event of an emergency and ran down the hall.

Once inside of her office, Denise began her search at Mona's desk and carefully shuffled her way through Mona's entire two-story, loft-style office. Annoyed beyond belief, Denise flopped down on the lounger. "Damn, maybe she took them home."

Just as Denise stood and made her way toward the door, her eyes traveled the length of the closet door to her right.

"Hmmm. I don't even remember seeing this door before."

Walking over toward the small closet, she switched on the light and walked inside. After 15 more minutes of snooping, she was tired, but she was finally rewarded. She found the tapes tucked deep in the back of Mona's walk-in closet in a small shoebox. Checking the time, Denise briskly made her way back to the receptionist area. She had just returned the key to the drawer and forged Jayme's name on the emergency key log just as the morning shift was walking in the door.

"Good morning, ladies," Denise said as she walked up to the entrance and turned the closed sign over to open. As soon as the coast was clear, she grabbed the tapes and shoved them in her purse.

Right before she zipped up her purse, she noticed a bright red and white piece of paper stuck to the bottom of one of the tapes. Ripping the paper from the center, Denise turned it over and tried to decipher the writing, but most of the note had been torn. She managed to read the last small part of the page:

'Love Shaun.'

Shaun? Just what the hell is this about and why was it in Mona's office?

****

So, that's why Carter told me to back off of Mona and why it was taking him so long to get his money back from her? Because he loves her? Why did he even accept my damn invitation to be more than fuck buddies if something was going on between them? I never got the impression that Shaun was ever with Mona, but a part of me always felt like he might've wanted to be.

Hollister walked into Bar 9 and couldn't wait to take a load off.

Grabbing a chair at the bar, he ordered a Heineken, a basket of hot wings, and tried to piece everything that's happened together since the day Shaun called and asked him to buy Mona out. *Maybe Carter did my car in, but he has no other motives. On the other hand, Shaun has all the motive, but I refuse to believe that my boy would do that. We've been cool for too long. Although, I never expected him to get as pissed off as he did when I backed out of the deal. But, I guess I'd be pissed too. But why do I have a feeling that there is more to this story than what Shaun told me?*

"Here are your wings, sir."

"Okay, thanks."

As Hollister ate his food, his thoughts kept going back to Mona. He really thought there was something there between them.

"Guess it was just my imagination," he mumbled.

But if she's with Carter, why did she agree to have dinner with me when she gets back in town? I guess we'll see. Tomorrow can't get here fast enough.

Hollister threw a fifty on the bar to cover his food, drink, and tip, then headed toward the men's restroom.

Halfway to his destination, he overheard a woman that looked vaguely familiar, talking eagerly on her phone. The mention of the name Mona made him slow his tracks some. He positioned himself within earshot and pulled his phone out and began playing with the screen, attempting to look busy.

"Hey baby, it was a little tricky, but no worries! I finally found and took what you needed from Mona's office. Now you can finally put that thieving bitch out of business for good. I bet she will *never* steal money from anyone else again. Anyway, I got to go for now, but I'll see you tonight. I love you, Shaun. Hope you're having a good day, baby. Bye."

When the mysterious woman ended the call, Hollister waited a few more minutes before he continued on to the restroom.

"I be damned, so Shaun really was telling the truth. He had to be, right?"

Overhearing that woman on the phone couldn't have been a coincidence, could it? Shaun, just what in the hell have you gotten me into, and what in the hell was on these so-called 'tapes' that she stole from Mona's office while she was out of town?

Peeking out the bathroom door, Hollister saw the woman receive her carryout and head for the exit. He waited a couple minutes, then he headed out making sure to stay on her tail. Outside, he walked right past her to his car and waited until she drove off before following a few cars behind her.

"I'm tired of being in the dark. I'm going to find out just how deep this bullshit goes."

****

Thirty minutes later, Hollister parked a few cars away from Denise in the Turn Ridge shopping plaza and watched as she entered Niko's Nail salon. He waited until the parking lot was practically empty before exiting his car and going over to her white Malibu. Peeking inside the back windows first and then the front, he looked around for a bag or box of any kind that the tapes could be in, but he saw nothing. Looking around again to make sure no one was watching him, Hollister took a chance and tried the passenger door.

He didn't hear Denise put on the alarm, so he assumed that there wasn't one or that she secured her car from the inside before she left. To his luck, the doors were unlocked and no alarm sounded. Quickly, Hollister had a look around, carefully checking the center console, then glove compartment, and finally under the seats. *Maybe they're in her purse.*

While climbing out of the car, he looked up and noticed that Denise was heading toward her car. Softly, he closed the door behind him, then went and stooped between two cars parked to the right side of her. Hollister listened as she laughed into her phone, while grabbing a piece of paper from the pocket in the side of her car door and ran back inside.

"Whew," Hollister said as he stood.

He was almost to his car when something told him to go back and check the trunk. Turning around, Hollister joggled back to the car, pressed in the button on the side of the driver's side door, and popped the truck. There in the corner was a small tote and sticking out of it were three tapes. Hollister reached for the bag when he heard heeled footsteps in the distance approaching fast. Popping his head up out of the trunk, he saw Denise coming back toward her car. Reaching inside the trunk, he swiped the handle of the bag when it snapped off and everything spilled out.

"Shit. Come on." He could hear her closing in on him, he grabbed the tape that had slid closest to his reach, closed the truck as quietly as he could, and ducked behind a black minivan, and as soon as Denise started her car, Hollister took off toward the opposite end of the lot.

****

"Hey baby, how was your—"

"Did you get them, where are the tapes?" Shaun appeared eager to skip the small talk.

"Hello, Shaun, how are *you*? Where are your manners?" Denise was irritated. She placed her handful of bags down on the kitchen table.

"I'm sorry. Hey baby, where are the tapes?" he asked as he placed a quick peck to her lips and started ransacking the bags.

"They're not in there, Shaun."

"Well, damnit, Denise! Where are they?" he raised his voice.

Walking over to her tote bag by the back door, Denise dug inside the bag and pulled out two tapes.

"Thank you, baby. Is this all of them?"

"Ye-yes."

"Why are you stuttering? Are there more?" Shaun said as he walked over to her and snatched the tapes from her hand.

"Shaun, was there ever anything between you and Mona?" Denise raised an eyebrow and met his eyes.

"Denise, I really don't have time for your fucking stupidity right now. Are there more goddamn tapes?"

"No. Those are it," she lied. "I've just never seen you so bent out of shape, is all." *The other one must still have fallen out of my bag and still be in my trunk somewhere, but I'm not about to tell him that.*

I'm sorry baby, but this entire situation got me so stressed out. I just want the bitch to give me what's mine."

"Well, calm down, you have everything you need now to close down that whore's shop and get back everything she owes you."

"And I owe it all to you." He smiled before heading toward his room.

"I'm going to make steaks and baked potatoes tonight, is that okay?" Denise asked.

"Yeah, whatever." Shaun slammed and locked his bedroom door behind him.

She pouted at his callous response. *What the hell is with him and why does he act like Dr. Jekyll & Ms. Hide when it comes to that thieving bitch? Oh, let me ask him about this damn piece of paper with his name on it before I forget.*

"Hey, baby? Baby? Shaun?" She knocked on the door.

"What Denise, damn?" He didn't open it.

"When is the last time you saw Mona?"

"I don't know, couple weeks ago, now leave me the hell alone. Please."

Shaking her head, Denise made her way back into the kitchen and began to prepare dinner. While moving the grocery bags from the table to the stovetop counter, she knocked a stack of Shaun's unopened mail to the floor.

Bending down, she neatly gathered all of the envelopes and papers into her hand when she came across an open bank statement and a particular purchase catching her eyes. *Roses, delivered to the Soothing Touch.*

He had never sent her anything while she worked at that place. Spreading the rest of the papers out on the floor, Mona flipped through the small pile looking for any other evidence that would prove exactly what she didn't want to believe. But there at the bottom of the pile was all the proof she needed that Shaun was in love with Mona and secretly trying to get her back.

"That bastard lied to me. He used and made a damn fool of me." She tore up the handwritten letter addressed to Mona, grabbed a dinner plate, and carefully placed the shreds of paper in it, then sat it on the table directly in front of his favorite chair and made her way toward his room.

"That bitch isn't the one for you, *I* am. She don't love you, *I* do. And it's about time that I show you just how much."

Chapter Sixteen

"Oh yesss. Carter." Mona was bent over the cream and bronze lounger on her tip toes, her ass high in the air. Carter stroked deep inside of her while simultaneously rubbing her clit with his thumb. They had been making love all over her suite all morning long and relentlessly going at each other like rabbits since his unexpected arrival.

"Fuck me, Carter...harder, baby," Mona moaned.

Carter didn't have to be told twice. He switched their position from the top of the lounger to the seat of it, slid back inside of her, and pummeled her sweet nectar until she was screaming and cumming all over his dick with shivering thighs.

"Ohhhh...Carterrrrr," Mona hoarsely moaned Carter's name when a thunderous sensation zapped through her clit and wet pussy and ping ponged throughout her body. Grinning, Carter didn't give Mona a second to recover. He flipped her over, scooted her to the end of the seat, spread her thighs wide, and dove deep inside of her drenched wet heat. He was holding her thighs in place while he slid in and out of her until she tried to scoot away.

"No, Carter, don't make me cum again."

"I won't, we're going to cum together," he grunted.

Carter then gripped her hips tight and alternated between dipping fast and slow inside of her. Kissing up and down her thighs and legs, he began a steady and calculated stroke while moving his right hand from her hips to fondle her nipples.

"Ohh...Carter." Mona was trying to slide away again to keep Carter constantly hitting her G-spot.

"Mona, don't move again, or I'll keep making you cum on my dick over and over again."

Mona tried to oblige, but the tingling that began in her toes was too powerful to keep still. Her moaning and the sweet steady increasing wetness was all he needed to let go.

"Awww shit. Yesss." He jerked his last few strokes, fighting to maintain composure.

Together, they came in unison before collapsing on the lounger.

"Carter, what are you *doing* to me?" Mona asked, damn near breathless.

"Me? I should be asking you that." He effortlessly grabbed Mona up, carried her out to the balcony and sat down on the oval loveseat, letting Mona sit in his lap.

"I have done nothing. I was minding my business, living my life. Then here you come wreaking havoc in my world."

"Wow, is that what I did?" Carter asked, smiling down into her beautiful brown eyes.

"Absolutely. And speaking of wreaking havoc in my world, you have taken over my entire vacation weekend. Today is my last day here in this beautiful city, and I'd actually like to see what the other side of my suite door is like, if that's okay with you."

"Alright, fine!" Carter grinned.

"Thank you," Mona said as she stood.

"Right after we wake the neighbors to the sight of you having an orgasm while bent over this balcony."

****

Shaun slammed his bedroom door shut and shook his head as he walked over to his dresser. "Got damn, I'm so sick of her ass. I can't wait until this shit is over."

Turning the tapes over in his hands, Shaun checked the brand to see if he had the camcorder already, or if he needed to buy a new one in the morning. Luckily, he had a Panasonic to match the tapes.

Shaun pulled his camera from the top shelf of his closet and put a tape inside. He turned on the camera and hit the play button. Immediately, the red room came into view and some moans could be heard soon after. As soon as he saw the image of another man's head between Mona's legs, he immediately got weak in the knees.

Taking a seat on the edge of his bed, he quickly ejected the tape and slid the next one in. This tape of the same man inside of her was his breaking point. He couldn't watch the scenes a second longer.

Turning off the camcorder, he sat it aside and laid in the bed on his back, the images still playing in his mind. He was so angry, he didn't know what to do. *How could she be so easy? How could she give up the goods to these nobodies and deny me a second chance?*

"It just doesn't seem like her at all. She would never do anything to jeopardize that parlor. She loved that place more than me. And she sure as hell doesn't like being recorded during sex."

The one time he tried, it didn't go over well at all. He thought back on the night he stopped having sex to grab the recorder, and she flipped out and made him go sleep on the couch. *Someone had to record her without her knowledge, but who?*

It didn't matter; he had what he needed to bribe her and take the parlor right out from under her. Shaun knew Mona would protect the Soothing Touch with her life, if need be. So now, he had the perfect bargaining chip to make her *his* again.

But who in the hell is this dude in the video? He could possibly become a problem...

Though he couldn't wait to set his plan into action, he had to find out as soon as possible who the guy was in the tape with Mona.

"Well, if dude becomes a problem, I'll just have to make sure he never becomes a problem again. Nobody fucks with my future."

****

"No this muthafucka didn't lock this damn door!" Denise turned Shaun's doorknob and it wouldn't budge.

"Shaun, why the hell you lock the door? I know you hear me

banging on this damn door. Shaun?!"

"Get the hell away from my door, Denise," Shaun spat from the other side.

"Oh, hell naw, he got me fucked all the way up."

She went to the kitchen and rumbled around inside of her purse until she found her nail file and Swiss army knife. Jogging back to Shaun's bedroom door, she stuck the shortest blade of the knife in the lock and the file through the side. After a few flips of her wrists, she heard the lock pop open. Pushing the door open, Denise walked inside the room and over to the bed where Shaun was sprawled next to an empty glass bottle of Hennessey Privilege in a half sleep, half-drunken stupor.

"Shaun? Why did you lock the door?"

"Go away, trying to sleep."

"Dinner is ready... you're not going to eat?" He was no good drunk like this. He wouldn't even remember her rant had she gone off on him.

"Get the hell out, Dee."

"Fine. I'll go, but stop fucking cussing at me, Shaun." She looked around the room until she spotted what she was looking for. She grabbed the tape from the floor and the recorder from the bed when Shaun rolled over onto his stomach.

"Get out and close the door."

"Fine. Whatever, you sorry ass lush."

Backing up into the hallway and away from him, she slowly placed her goodies on the floor in the hallway.

When she turned back and got ready to close the door, Shaun mumbled something. Stepping back into the room, she heard him clear as day.

"Go get my Mona. I want her back, want to make her my wife..."

Denise walked out the room and slammed the door behind her.

"Fucking lying bastard." She made her way to the kitchen, grabbed up her purse, and made a beeline for the door.

"Oh no, you ain't going to make no bitch your mutherfuckin' wife but me, and I'm about to make absolutely certain of that. Time to get rid of this uppity bitch for good."

Chapter Seventeen

Hollister sped all the way across town to the eastside to his mother's house. Straight to the basement he went, and he didn't stop until he reached the storage room.

Looking up on the top shelf, he spotted the camcorder that he knew his parents kept here. Praying the batteries still had some juice, he switched on the power button and it instantly turned green.

"Thank you, God," Hollister said as he pulled the tape out of his pocket, popped it into the camera, and pressed play. Even though he was actually seeing the proof with his own eyes, he still couldn't believe Mona was with Carter, and that she was actually fucking him on the job.

"You don't look so legitimate now, do you Mona? So, Carter had been playing me the entire time, huh? Well, this definitely calls for an even scoreboard."

****

Mona strolled back into her parlor early Monday morning smiling from ear to ear and humming *Beg for It* by Chris Brown. She was feeling absolutely fantastic. She was about to break out in dance and skip all the way to her office when her phone started chirping.

"Hello? *Hello*?" After a third hello, she ended the call. "And this is exactly why I don't answer numbers I don't recognize," Mona said annoyed.

Dropping her phone in her purse, she continued to her office but stopped when she heard a noise. She turned around, but saw nothing. Mona listened for the sound again. Still nothing.

Turing back around, she walked back to the back door to make sure she'd closed it behind her. She opened the door, looked around, and closed and locked it behind her. She then went and did the same thing to the front door. By the time Mona had finally made it inside of her office, she'd felt like she was starring in a made for television horror flick.

Closing her office door behind her, Mona put her bags away and immediately got to work. After catching up on paperwork, orders, appointments, special events, and promotions, it was almost time to open up for business. She inspected her rooms one more time, checking every room for accuracy and cleanliness. When everything was satisfactory, Mona heard her day shift clocking in for work.

"Hello, ladies."

"Good morning, Mona, welcome back. How was your vacation?" the ladies asked.

"Oh, it was absolutely wonderful. I had an amazing time." Mona reached up to flip the closed sign over and unlock the doors.

"Well, someone got their socks knocked off in Key West." Jayme grinned as he made her way around the hostess stand.

"Maybe I did, maybe I didn't. Bad girls never tell." Mona winked and left the ladies to their light opening duties.

Back in her office, she made a mental note to call her cousin, Phyllis, back and remind her not to go through with the plans to send the tapes to the news, which reminded her to get rid of the evidence she had herself once and for all.

Let me get rid of these tapes before I forget.

All this blackmail wasn't in her character. She was so glad everything was over. She walked over to the closet and knelt down to search for her last damning secret.

"Uhh, Officer. *Please!* Just let us get our boss! Don't treat the customers that way!"

She could hear footsteps rapidly approaching her office door.

"Mona!" Jayme knocked rapidly as Mona opened the door. "Come on. Something is going on—the police—"

Running out of her office, Mona rounded the corner and saw two police officers escorting her customers out of her place.

"Excuse me! Hey, just what in the hell do you think that you are doing?" Mona walked up to the big burley officer that was standing in the middle of her parlor barking out orders.

"Are you Mona Carwtright?"

"What's it to you, jerk? And I'm not answering your question until you answer mine! Who sent you here? What is this about?!"

"I'll take that as a yes. Miss Mona Cartwright, you are under arrest for solicitation of sex for money and heading up and running a prostitution ring under the disguise of a legitimate business." The officer spun her around and cuffed her hands behind her back. He then proceeded to read her the rest of her Miranda rights as he led her to his squad car.

****

"Mona, what the hell is going on? You and your parlor—it's all over the news. What happened?" Carter asked as they descended the steps of the police station.

"I don't know what the hell is going on."

"Mona, I don't believe you, and I don't know what the hell is going on, but this is where I get the fuck off this ride."

"Carter, I didn't do this, why don't you believe me?"

"It doesn't matter, if you had never tried to get even—If you would have just fuckin' asked me what the hell was going on, we wouldn't be standing here right now and I wouldn't have lost everything. What the hell am I supposed to do, Mona?"

"I lost everything too, Carter."

"You know what, that victim shit is played out. Have a nice life, Mona."

"Carter. Carter, c'mon. Caarrttteerrrr!!?"

He was already walking in the opposite direction and never looked back. Angry, Mona sat on the ledge of the wall of the police station looking around for Trina and trying not to cry. She couldn't believe Carter just flipped on her. She knew her cousin would never leak those tapes when she asked her not to. But if Phyllis didn't do it, who in the hell did?" *Who hated me this much that they would do this to me?*

Mona couldn't hold the tears that had been threatening to fall for the last five minutes. Sobbing into her hands, Mona cried from her soul, she couldn't believe that her life had come to this. All she had worked for was circling the drain.

"Mona?"

Snapping her head up, Mona glanced in the direction she heard her name being called and froze at the sight of Hollister.

"What the hell do you want, Hollister?"

"Can we talk?"

"Hollister, I never want to talk to you or see you again. I know all about your hand in trying to ruin my business. Don't ever speak to or come near me again." She stood to make her way toward the other side of the police station.

"Mona, it's not what you think. If you would just let me explain…"

"It's so funny how everyone wants to *explain* now that my business is officially under fuckin' investigation. I've lost the trust of my customers and now my name means mud. You had plenty of time to explain whatever the hell you wanted from me a long time ago.

Goodbye, Hollister."

"Mona, you're right, and I'm sorry, but if you'd just let me tell you how Shaun got me in this mess, you'd—"

"Shaun, Shaun Harper?"

"Yes."

"How do you know Shaun, Hollister?"

"Let me drive you home and I'll explain everything."

She was reluctant, but desperate, and flailing for air. "Okay."

"Alright, let me run and get my car and I'll be right back."

As Mona watched Hollister run across the street, her head was spinning. She didn't know how many more secrets and lies she could take.

Hollister had just pulled up, jumped out of the car, and opened the door for Mona when somewhere in the distance, she heard someone call her name. She turned to look behind her, but there was no one there.

Shaking off the weird vibes she was getting, Mona eased into the passenger seat, feeling like the weight of the world was on her shoulders. As Hollister pulled off, Mona closed her eyes and prayed that all of this was all a bad dream.

Chapter Eighteen

Denise sat in her car across the street from the police station laughing her head off until she saw Shaun speed up trying to catch up to Mona by hysterically yelling and waving his hands trying to get her attention. Grinning devilishly, Denise began clapping like a kid getting candy when the driver of the car Mona had gotten in, sped off and rounded the corner. Her grin was wide as Shaun too lost sight of them.

"Now Shaun, we really need to work on our communication skills honey, 'cause I could've sworn that you told me you would be out of town all week. But that's okay, I'll help you with your little communication problem if it's the last thing I do."

Denise grabbed her purse and pulled her gun from its holster. Checking the chamber, she emptied two of the six bullets into her hand and popped it back in place. Sitting the gun in her lap, she waited until Shaun drove off.

Don't worry, Shaun, I'm going to fix our little problem for good this time. When that scrawny bitch is dead, you'll come to your senses. And to my bed... She fingered the gun as it sat in the passenger side, shiny and cold. Up until now, it had been nothing more than a toy for her to play with at the shooting range.

"You don't promise me forever, Shaun. It doesn't work that way."

****

"I *stole* from him? Is that what he's telling people now? Let me tell you something, Hollister, I never stole a dime from your *friend*. And we were never business partners. We used to date, but shit got too serious for him and *he* left *me*. His shady ass broke up with me over a text message. I can't believe that he's really behind all this! And I bet he leaked those tapes because I wouldn't get back together with him. Fucking bastard! Hollister. hurry up and get me home please, because I'm going to pay back this sick ass son of a bitch tonight."

"Mona. I honestly don't know how much of this is actually his doing because like I told you, I stole one of the tapes from some woman's truck. I mean, it's all fishy, but he's definitely got something to do with this." He turned right off I-94 and Ten Mile.

"I can't believe that he would do this to me. I have done nothing to him but forgiven him. I told him to his face to move on. That I wasn't interested in another chance. I wanted him to be happy, too." She shook her head at the thought of desperation Shaun had shown, manipulating her dreams and sabotaging her life and her *lover's*.

"Does he really think that *this* will win me over? He's fuckin' insane!"

"And that's why I don't think you should confront him tonight and definitely not without the police or somebody that can take his ass out, if need be. Listen Mona, the next morning after I backed out of our deal, my car wouldn't start. I found out when I got to the mechanic, that it was intentionally tampered with. I could've been killed. I know it had to be his crazy ass, but I didn't wanna believe it. We were boys for so long..."

"Well, I'm not you, Hollister, and I'm through givin' a fuck. I mean, why are you spilling the beans now? It ain't exactly like you're innocent in all this! I should turn your ass in too when this is all said and done."

"Mona look, I can't undo all that has happened, I can only do what I can to make things right, now. Believe it or not, I've grown to care for you deeply and under different circumstances, I would have loved to see where things could have gone with us. I was so fucking pissed at you, Shaun and Carter, that y'all *all* almost came up missing. Hell, Carter and Shaun still might—but with you, I just wanted to come clean and do whatever I could to see that smile light up your face. And maybe one day, if ever you can forgive me in my part in all this craziness, we could become friends, or who knows, something more."

He pulled into Mona's driveway and cut his engine. He looked over at Mona as she stared out of the window, no doubt deep in thought. After a few moments, he reached for her hand and closed his hand around it. Surprisingly, she didn't pull away.

"Thanks for the ride home, Hollister. Thanks for everything tonight."

"Sure thing. I meant every word I said. And if you'd let me, I wanna help you fix all this."

****

Exhausted, Mona stripped down to her t-shirt, panties, and bare feet and slowly moved to the shower. She had just drawn the shower curtain closed when her doorbell rang and a soft knock sounded at her door. Thinking it was Hollister, she cracked open the door without checking her peephole. "What, did I leave something in your—"

"Hello, Mona Lisa. May I come inside and talk?"

"Can you come in and *talk*? After everything that I just found out that you've done to me? You couldn't even come inside of my house if you were on fire and I was the only one on the block who had enough water to put you out. Now get the hell away from my door..."

"If you try to close the door, bitch, you'll be dead before it clicks shut. Now open the fucking door and back the fuck up. And if I were you, I would move quickly."

Mona backed up, her hands in the surrender position as Denise brushed past Shaun with her pistol in her hand, aimed right at Mona.

"D-Denise, what the hell are you doing here? What the fuck is all this?"

"Yeah, Dee-Dee, what the hell is going on?" Shaun asked confused as he slowly stepped inside of Mona's home but stayed close to the door. He had no idea she had followed him to Mona's.

"I'm doing what you should've done a long time ago when this bitch stole from you. It's taken you too long to get your money back and get this bitch out of our lives. Now go get everything of value out of this trash dump of a house, so we can get the hell on and *finally* be together." Denise held the gun like a pro, her gaze never leaving Mona's terrified face. Her hands never wavered. She looked completely in control.

"Dee-Dee, I have the situation under control, please put the gun down before—"

Denise fired a single shot up into the ceiling to get Shaun's attention. "No, we do things *my* way from here on out. Now move Shaun before the cops get word. Go get her shit and let's get out of here."

Mona watched in utter disbelief and disgust as Shaun went on a shopping spree in her castle. She was being held up by her own *employee*, while her *ex* looted her place for everything she'd worked so hard for. She had to get the truth out.

"Look Denise, I don't know what the hell Shaun told you, but it was all lies. I haven't stolen anything from him. This is his twisted way of trying to get back with me."

"No. Shut the fuck up. Shaun wouldn't lie to me. He doesn't want you—he wants *me*. Us. He promised me that we could finally be together just as soon as he got his money back from you. He said he would use the money to buy me a ring and us a big house in Grosse Pointe Farms. And just so we are clear, Shaun didn't leak those tapes, *I* did. I broke into your office and stole them from you—out of that little closet you think no one sees. I only took the job at your whore house parlor to help my man because he asked me to."

Shaun came down the stairs with Mona's things in a big garbage bag. He'd only caught the tail end of the conversation. "Denise, why did you leak the tapes? I *told* you I had everything under control."

"Shaun, you had nothing under control. I mean, look at us. You were too busy under this bitches spell. I couldn't let you let this bitch make you forget about me and all that you promised me, baby."

"You can have him. You two fuckin' belong together."

"Shut the fuck up, Mona. He's already mine."

"Okay, look baby. We can go now. Look—we have everything we need." He showed Denise the bag full of money, jewelry and other small electronics that she kept for business purposes. Her iPad minis, Bluetooth stereos, all of her back-up equipment was on display for Denise while she kept that gun pointed at Mona's face.

"I got all the money from her safe I found in her den and all her jewelry and valuables that she owns. So, let's roll out baby before the cops pull up. I think I can hear some sirens in the distance."

"Okay, but one more thing first. Did you really used to date her?"

Shaun glanced out of the window and sighed deeply before he finally answered, "At one point in time, yes."

"She said you were trying to get back with her. Is that true, Shaun?"

"N-no. Not at all. Whatever she told you is all lies."

"No they're not. Denise, you have got to believe me. He sent me flowers and came by my house to talk."

"She's lying."

"I'm not, I have proof. He dropped his watch when he left. It's on my kitchen table. Can I go get it?"

"No, she's lying. She'll run," Shaun said.

Panic appeared on his face. He stood there looking like he'd just seen a ghost.

"I'm not a liar like you, you sorry, thieving, bastard."

"Hey, shut the fuck up now. Both of you. Here, shoot her," Denise said as she pulled another gun from the waistband of her jeans.

"What?" Shaun looked in horror at the second gun.

"If she's lying, shoot her. In the heart."

"Denise, I don't want a case over this lying—"

"Goddamn it, Shaun. If the bitch is lying, shoot her!" Holding the gun out to him, Denise waited until he cradled it into his hand slowly aimed it at Mona.

"Wait, I got a better idea. Let's just shoot her together, baby. Okay?"

"A-alright."

"Okay. On the count of three."

Mona was now looking down the barrel of two guns. She couldn't believe she was going out like this...

"1...2...3..."

Denise pulled the trigger but didn't see if the bullet pierced Mona's heart as planned because she was tackled to the ground from behind. As soon as her and her attacker hit the floor, Shaun dropped his gun and ran out the door.

"Get the fuck off of me!!"

"Hell naw, psycho!" They both wrestled relentlessly, scrambling for the gun that had been kicked across the room.

Carter had never hit a woman in his life, but he had to do something quick because both he and Mona would soon be dead if he didn't. Since Denise had no problem firing punches and swift kicks into his side, Carter kneed her in the side and bent her arms behind her back. Denise somehow managed to kick him in the nuts and back.

"Fuck!" Carter yelled as he loosened his grab on her arms and she scrambled away. Carter lunged for her, reached out and caught her leg and twisted in until he heard it snap.

"Aghhhh!" Denise screamed as he rolled over. Carter didn't see the gun in her hand, but he did remember looking into the barrel of the gun before he heard a loud deafening pop. He fell to his back and closed his eyes and listened as the sirens became louder…

****

Mona sat up in her beach lounger and looked out into the clear blue beach waters of Key West under a breathtaking soft orange and indigo sky.

"How're you feeling sexy?"

"Like the luckiest man in the world. What about you, beautiful?" Carter sat up in his lounger and threw his long legs over the side.

"Like the luckiest woman in the world. Good. You ready to go in?"

"Naw, not yet, I have to see the sun go down first."

"Okay, well come sit on my lap and let me hold you while it goes down."

Mona's smile rivaled the beautiful late evening sky as she snuggled close to Carter.

"So, do you think you'll be ready to go back to work anytime soon?"

"Nah, I've decided to let Hollister sell the parlor for me when we get back."

"Well, whatever you do, you'll always have my support. There isn't a day that goes by that I don't think about the night I looked down the barrel of that gun and you came to my rescue."

"I still cry about that every night. I've never taken a life before, but if I hadn't pulled the trigger, neither of us would be here. I hate that Denise ended up dying at the hospital."

"Yeah, me too. I wanted her to rot in prison."

"Carter..." His words were unsettling.

"*What*? Mona, I have no sympathy for that woman after what she was about to do to us. None, and I never will. And if Shaun's punk ass hadn't confessed, I would've hunted his ass down and beat him to death myself. And the only reason that I'm not fucking Hollister up on site is because you begged me not to."

"Well, I'm just glad it's all over and that I'm finally with the man

I love."

"I'll tell you one thing, though. I'm going to miss the Red Room something terrible."

"Me too," Mona laughed.

"What do you say we add an addition on to my house and you recreate the Red Room just for us?"

"Now that sounds like a plan, baby."

"Good. I'll get construction started on it as soon as we're done traveling the world."

"I can't wait, but if you don't mind, could you slightly alter the new room for me?"

"What did you have in mind?" Carter asked as he pulled her even closer.

"Could you put a floor to ceiling window in place of one of the walls so we can watch beautiful sunsets just like this one?"

"Absolutely, Ms. Cartwright. Anything for you."

Made in the USA
Columbia, SC
26 May 2017